Benjamin Constant

BENJAMIN CONSTANT, French writer and politician, was born in Lausanne on October 25, 1767, and died in Paris on December 8, 1830. He combined an extraordinarily lively political career with fertile literary output and an enthusiastic series of liaisons with some of France's most prominent women. Among them were two of his mistresses, Madame de Staël and Madame Récamier, and his two wives, Wilhelmina, Baroness Chramm and Charlotte von Hardenberg. Constant received the education typical of a well-fixed, upper-class young man of his time. He studied in Brussels, Oxford, Erlangen and Edinburgh, and was then appointed chamberlain in the court of Charles William, duke of Brunswick. Although a liberal monarchist for most of his life, in 1841 he switched sides in favor of Napoleon and was driven into exile when Louis XVIII returned to the throne. His political fortunes subsequently improved and at his death he was president of the council of State. Constant was an ardent champion of freedom of the press, the author of a substantial number of books including novels, political tracts and a massive history of religion, and a man who responded vitally to the opportunities and challenges of his century.

Benjamin Constant

ADOLPHE

AND

THE RED NOTEBOOK

WITH AN INTRODUCTION BY
HAROLD NICOLSON

A SIGNET  CLASSIC

Published by

THE NEW AMERICAN LIBRARY

First Printing, August, 1959

SIGNET CLASSICS *are published by*
The New American Library of World Literature, Inc.
501 Madison Avenue, New York 22, New York

PRINTED IN THE UNITED STATES OF AMERICA

Contents

Introduction

I

To UNDERSTAND *Adolphe* and to appreciate the mood in which it was written, it is necessary to know something of the life and love-affairs of Benjamin Constant, and to realize the conflict within him between the artist and the man of action. *Adolphe* essentially is an autobiographical novel; but it is neither a complete self-portrait, nor a direct description of the woman by whom, in his middle years, he was dominated and controlled. It represents Constant during that phase of his life when he was torn between pity, subservience, and a desire to escape. Under the transparent disguise of an affair with Anna Lindsay, he describes how the bond which had been forged between him and Madame de Stael had grown, link by link, into a rusted chain of iron.

In *The Red Notebook*—a slim book of 227 written pages, bound in red paper and first published in 1907—Constant has given his own account of the first twenty years of his life. Yet if we are to estimate the curious blending in his character of the purposeful and the haphazard, of the selfish and the self-sacrificing, of ambition and sentiment, of impulsiveness and diffidence; if, that is, we are to acquire any comprehension of his strangely dual temperament; it is necessary to supplement his own account from other and perhaps more objective sources.

Henri Benjamin Constant de Rebecque was born at Lausanne in Switzerland on 25 October 1767. The house, which until 1912 was still standing in the Rue du Grand-Chêne, was a long, low building of two stories with high windows opening upon the chestnuts of a little garden. His mother, Henrietta de Chandieu, died a few days after his birth. His grandmother and his aunt, Madame de Nassau, strove to secure the charge of this motherless infant: his father wished to keep the boy for himself. 'He was', as his cousin Rosalie wrote in later years, 'regarded by the family as a fragile but precious object, of which each in turn desired to obtain possession.' But the father won.

Colonel Juste de Constant is vividly depicted both in the *Cahier Rouge* and in *Adolphe* itself. He combined the tolerance of the eighteenth century with a cold Protestantism. While condoning the follies of his son, while encouraging his vices, he was unable (perhaps from secret shyness) to accord him either his confidence or his affection. Although he possessed several different properties in Switzerland, he preferred to take service in the Swiss regiment in the Low Countries. He was always on the move between the Lake of Geneva, Brussels, Germany and the garrison towns of the Netherlands. Before his marriage to Benjamin's mother he had taken charge of a little girl of nine, whose real name was Jeanne Mangin, but who was subsequently known as 'Marianne.' He educated this child according to his own theories, and eventually she became his housekeeper and his second wife. It was to her simple care that the young Benjamin was first entrusted. In later years Colonel de Constant, much to Benjamin's distress, became involved in a lawsuit with the officers of his own regiment. He failed to win either the lawsuit or the expensive appeal which he thereafter lodged. He lost his job and had to sell most of his properties. He died a discontented man.

Benjamin's childhood years were spent in one or other of the family houses which fringed the shores of the Lake of Geneva. He was given French tutors, German tutors and English tutors; these pedagogues seem to have been selected almost by chance and without discrimination. Benjamin was a precocious child; he mastered the rudiments of Greek grammar at the age of five; the letters which he wrote at the age of ten are so mature that Sainte-Beuve (who detested Benjamin Constant and sought always to discredit him) pronounced them to be forgeries. They were, in fact, authentic. 'I wish', he wrote while still a little boy, 'that someone could stop my blood circulating so rapidly and impart to it a calmer rhythm. I have tried to see whether music could produce this effect; I have been playing adagios and largos such as would send thirty cardinals to sleep.' The feverish impatience, which in adult years amounted to a gambler's recklessness, was a cause of worry to Benjamin even as a child. His father did little to render him more quiescent. He dragged him off to Paris, he took him over to Oxford for a while, he sent him to the German university of Erlangen. From Germany, on a sudden impulse, Benjamin went to Edinburgh where he enrolled himself as a student. The year and a half which he spent in Scotland appeared to him in later life as the happiest of all his many interludes. In 1786, at the age of nineteen, he crossed again to Paris; there followed a period of gaming and debauchery; and it was then that he met the first of the three women who were to dominate his life.

Madame de Charrière at that date was forty-seven years of age: she is the 'Zélide' of Geoffrey Scott's delicate biography. As a girl of some beauty and great gifts she had had many suitors, including James Boswell and Benjamin's uncle. But in the end she married M. de Charrière, her brother's dull but worthy tutor, and with him she retired to the estate of Colombiers, near Neuchâtel. She acquired a certain literary reputation by her novel *Caliste* and her *Lettres de Lausanne;* she possessed a logical eighteenth-century mind, considerable powers of conversation, a taste for opium, and a capacity for deep maternal affection. Constant accompanied her from Paris to Colombiers, where he started writing his *History of Religion,* the final version of which was not published for forty years. At Colombiers Constant found many of the things that he needed; seclusion, since at that time he was suffering from an unfortunate malady which developed into skin disease; that maternal affection of which fate had deprived him; and infinite opportunities for conversation. They would sit there by the stove in Madame de Charrière's drawing-room, under the heavy Pompeian decoration of the domed ceiling, and exchange general ideas until the dawn showed through the shutters. She became his mentor and his confidante: in *Adolphe* she appears as a peaceful memory in the passages which occur in Chapter I.

Constant's platonic, but not unemotional, friendship

with Madame de Charrière lasted for almost ten years, from 1786 to 1795. With her he found protection without captivity, firmness without rage. While she ruled his life he was free to indulge in other employments and to contract other affections. There was Mrs. Trevor, the wife of the British Minister at Turin, a coquette of mature years who rejected his vigorous but timid advances. There was Jenny Pourras, a young heiress who refused to marry him; at which, and not for the last time, he staged a mock suicide. In 1788, while he was still suffering from herpes, his father, resenting what he imagined to be the idleness of Colombiers, packed him off to the Court of Brunswick, having obtained for him a post of junior chamberlain. The next year Benjamin startled them all by marrying Baroness Minna von Cramm, one of the ladies of the ducal court, who possessed neither beauty, charm, nor character. After a few months of bitter wrangling they agreed to separate; Minna was not only unfaithful to him, she also disclosed to the Duke of Brunswick certain writings of Constant in which his employers were exposed to ridicule; he thus lost his job and his wife at the same time. They were divorced in March 1793 and Constant returned to Colombiers to nurse his wounds.

Madame de Charrière had always realized that the influence which she exercised upon the young Constant was protective and intellectual; she called it her 'intellectual maternity'. She had not, for this reason, been jealous of Mrs. Trevor, or Jenny Pourras, or even of Minna von Cramm; she knew that she could provide him with something which they could never supply. But she was terrified of Madame de Stael. Here was a potential rival, twenty-six years younger than herself, abounding in vitality, rich, managing, famous, and endowed with a capacity for conversation in comparison to which the talks at Colombiers would seem but faint logical murmurs beside a stove. In her letters she sought to discredit her formidable successor in the eyes of Benjamin. How vulgar was Madame de Stael, how inelegant, how snobbish, how essentially silly. 'She is not', wrote Zélide, 'authentic.' But in her lonely, unhappy heart, Madame de Charrière knew that in the end the two must meet; and that her Benjamin would at once be captured and enslaved.

II

ON A SEPTEMBER MORNING in 1794 Madame de Stael was driving along the road from Coppet to Mézery. Her carriage was intercepted by a young man on horseback who explained that he has just been to Coppet and had been told by her servants that she had left but an hour before; he had thus cantered along the road to catch her up. She invited him to enter her carriage; at once they embarked upon a tremendous discussion regarding the liberty of the press.

Benjamin Constant at that date was twenty-seven years of age. His appearance was not prepossessing. His carroty hair hung over his forehead in wisps, his white face was blotched with yellow patches; his little eyes glinted within half-closed eyelids and behind green spectacles; his lips were mobile and slim. He had a weedy body, and white freckled hands which jerked nervously; his finger was constantly in his mouth. He had a thin, rather effeminate voice, and when he uttered his epigrams, the sibilants hissed and whistled.

Constant returned to Coppet with Madame de Stael. Madame de Charrière sought for a moment to brave it out. 'What fun we shall have', she wrote pathetically, 'laughing at her when you return.' 'It seems to me,' replied Constant, 'that you judge her too severely.' This letter had been written on a paper scented with ambergris. Madame de Charrière was too intelligent a woman not to realize that she was beaten. 'Benjamin,' she replied, 'you are beginning to take pains about your personal appearance; you no longer love me.' Constant, in a mood of ruthless impatience, decided to confess that he had fallen in love with Madame de Stael. 'She is', he wrote to Zélide, 'the second woman in my life who could fill my whole universe; you know who was the first.' The reign of Madame de Charrière had ended: the tyranny of Germaine de Stael had begun.

The subsequent stages of Constant's enslavement are

comprehensible; we can find in them a combination of mixed motives and emotions: intellectual admiration and enjoyment, habit, convenience, vanity, a need for mental excitement, gratitude, duty, worldly ambition, compassion, and sheer physical and nervous terror. It is the sudden and overwhelming infatuation of the first months that is so difficult to explain. Madame de Stael, even at the age of twenty-eight, was not an attractive woman. Her figure was ungainly, her skin tawny, her gestures violent, her voice loud and hoarse. It may be that, like Adolphe, Constant possessed the gambler's reckless desire for immediate acquisition. It may be also that, as so often happens with neurotics, he was less in love with an individual than in love with love. It may be that, being conscious of his own sexual timidity, he forced himself into positions more extreme and inevitable than a less cerebral sensualist would need to adopt. And it may be again that, mortified as he was by his own lack of physical attraction, detecting in the eyes of Madame de Stael the repulsion which he inspired, he forced himself to stake everything on win or lose.

He was certainly impulsive. A few hours only after his arrival at Coppet he began to display marked symptoms of physical passion. Madame de Stael rejected his advances. He resorted to his former trick of attempted suicide; he swallowed opium, roused the household, and insisted that Madame de Stael should come to him before he expired. 'Tell her', he panted, 'that it is from love of her that I die.' Madame de Stael, roused from her slumbers, hurried to his bedside; he covered her hand with kisses and almost immediately recovered. When she returned to her own room she plunged into scented water the hand that he had kissed. 'I feel for that man', she confessed, 'a physical antipathy which nothing can surmount.'

Within a few days Constant was convalescent. She allowed him to sit up with her until midnight had struck. One night he overstayed the time allotted to him and she told him to consult his watch. It was ten minutes after midnight. He took the watch and smashed it against the marble mantelpiece. This gesture seems to have had more effect upon the Baroness than the attempted suicide. Next morning Constant notes in his diary: 'I shall not buy another watch. I have no longer any need of it.'

Madame de Stael was the most possessive woman that ever lived. None of her victims was ever allowed to leave the gilded cage. She forced them to sign acts of capitulation under which they bound themselves to eternal fidelity and obedience. If any of them managed to escape for a moment, one of the other victims, or even her own son, was sent after the renegade to fetch him back. The discipline she imposed was ferocious; the scenes she enacted were uncontrolled; she would rush like a maenad along the passages with foam upon her lips; the placid waters of Lac Leman echoed to her hoarse and frenzied cries. The prisoners themselves, in spite of their mutual antipathy, huddled like cows together in a common fear.

The Coppet establishment has often been described. The permanent prisoners, apart from Constant himself, were Mathieu de Montmorency, Schlegel, the banker Sismondi, Elzear de Sabran and Prosper de Barante. The only women inhabitants were Madame Necker de Saussure and Madame Récamier. They all met at breakfast at eight in the morning; conversation then continued for three-and-a-half hours until the midday meal; there was a pause till dinner when conversation was resumed. From time to time there would be amateur theatricals, at which Madame de Stael excelled in the part of Phèdre. The lack of privacy must have been appalling; there were no locks to the doors and Madame de Stael, armed with her green morocco writing case, would burst into the rooms of her victims at any hour of the day and night, shouting incessantly, often in rage. Occasionally they would all go on expeditions together or undertake voyages to Germany or France. Vociferous and untiring, Madame de Stael lashed out at her troop of galley slaves. They bowed their head in admiration, anger and shame.

III

IN MAY 1795 MADAME DE STAEL had felt that it was safe to return to Paris and to reopen her salon. She brought Benjamin with her. When the Directory was established a few months later they imagined that their opportunity had come. The frenzy of the Revolution had spent itself; a new epoch of philosophic liberalism was about to open; and under such a system they would both, with their intellectual energies and their uncompromised pasts, find scope for their ambitions. Benjamin would play the part of a liberal politician, perhaps even of a statesman; and Madame de Stael from her salon would become the tutelary goddess of the whole movement. Their hopes were disappointed. Benjamin presented himself to the electors, but, owing to his Swiss origin, he was not returned; and Madame de Stael aroused hostility by her arrogance, and suspicion by her unbridled tactlessness. 'One is no more', she confessed, 'than a pebble thrown into an enormous wheel.'

And then came the 18 Brumaire and the advent of Bonaparte. Madame de Stael loved liberty, but she worshipped power. She spared no pains to flatter Bonaparte and to obtain a place for Benjamin. Somewhat contemptuously the First Consul appointed Benjamin Constant as the representative in the Tribunate for the Department of Leman. 'After all,' he is reported to have said, 'why not?' But Madame de Stael was as unable to keep silent as Constant was unable to refrain from criticism. Bonaparte soon lost his patience. In 1802 Constant was deprived of his job in the Tribunate and Madame de Stael was ordered to leave Paris. So far from having assisted him in his ambitions, Madame de Stael, by her chatter and self-assertion, had ruined his political career. They returned to Coppet, mortified and resentful. The only function that remained to them was to become the twin martyrs of Bonapartism.

The infatuation which had swept Constant off his balance in 1794 had not been of long duration; within a few months the lover had become the servant. So long ago as May 1797 he had confessed to his aunt, Madame de Nassau, that 'a bond by which I am held, owing to a sense of duty, or, if you prefer it, from weakness, renders me profoundly unhappy.' With the destruction of his political ambitions, this bond became increasingly irksome. Moreover, while in Paris in 1800, he had fallen in love with someone else.

Anna Lindsay, known officially as Madame Lindsay, had been born in 1764, the daughter of an Irish inn-keeper at Calais of the name of Jeremy O'Dwyer. While still a girl she had attracted the attention of the Duchess of Fitz-James who had removed her from her father's inn, given her some education and a taste for elegance, and then left her to her own devices. After an early life of varied gallantry, she had formed in 1788 a serious connection with Auguste de Lamoignon, by whom she had two children. She possessed a domestic nature and a longing to become respectable; her personal charm, the services which during the Revolution she had been able to render to the *émigrés*, and her long fidelity to Lamoignon, enabled her to create a place for herself on the fringes of the tolerant society of the Directory. It was Julie Talma, Constant's devoted friend, who brought the two together in October 1800. Benjamin was thirty-two at that date and Madame Lindsay was thirty-six; he had always preferred women older than himself. He fell in love with her and she gave herself to him within a few days of their first meeting. It was customary for Constant to tire of a thing the moment he had come to possess it; the honeymoon with Anna Lindsay was prolonged by the stimulating circumstance that possession could not be absolute. She was tied by her duty towards Lamoignon; he by his service to Madame de Stael. An element of uncertainty was thus introduced into their relationship; and this tension postponed for Benjamin the advent of satiety. This early period is described in the famous, and indeed striking, opening to Chapter IV. Constant, during the blaze of his early passion, urged Madame Lindsay to break with Lamoignon, and promised that if she did so, he would sever his connection with Madame de Stael. Within a few months, however, he had thought much better of this proposal. Not only would it be difficult, and even dangerous, to escape from Madame de Stael's clutches, but if Lamoignon ceased to be responsible for Anna Lindsay, then Constant might have to support both her and the two children himself. He poured out his perplexity to Madame Talma. She was sympathetic, helpful, but a shade too frank. Julie Talma was a penetrating woman. She understood Benjamin Constant better even than he understood himself. Her nickname for him was *'la vieille coquette'*. Behind all his ecstatics she detected the exasperation wrought in him by the conflict between his artistic sensibility and his desire to appear as the man of action, irresistible and passionate. She foresaw the reaction which possession was bound to produce. 'What you would like to do', she wrote to him a trifle harshly, 'is to seduce women: but you can only charm them.' The letters which Constant wrote to Madame Lindsay did not seem to Madame Talma to be honest or fair. 'They are a mixture', she wrote, 'of passion and indifference; of the outspoken and the sly; half of what they contain induces despair; the other half inspires hope.' So long as Madame Talma was alive the affair between Constant and Madame Lindsay pursued its complicated and neurotic course. But Madame Talma died in May 1805; and thereafter Constant returned to Coppet and did not see Anna Lindsay for a space of ten years. Mortified, unhappy, and disgusted with his own wretched weakness, he resumed his former servitude. And it was in such a mood, in the late autumn of 1806, that he wrote *Adolphe*.

IV

IN 1801, MONSIEUR DE STAEL, the dim but official husband of the Baroness, had died of apoplexy. Constant felt that it was obligatory to suggest marriage to his widow. She refused, on the sensible ground that it would be foolish at her age to change a name which she had rendered so famous. In 1804 a further entanglement occurred. Monsieur Necker, the father for whom Madame de Stael entertained so extravagant a passion, died at Coppet. Her desolation at this misfortune was not feigned; Constant felt obliged to comfort and assuage her by any means in his power. This added a further link to his chain. By 1806, however, this link also had become rusted. It must be realized that *Adolphe* was written at a moment when Constant was ruminating, was even planning, the most intricate and excruciating manœuvres for escape. 'I am tired', he wrote, 'of being always necessary and never adequate.' 'Benjamin', wrote Madame de

Stael, 'is too incomplete, both in feeling and in character, to suffice me wholly.'

He began to write *Adolphe* in the autumn of 1806. 'Benjamin', Madame de Stael informed Bonstetten on 15 November of that year, 'has begun a novel, which is the most original and the most moving of any I have read.' It may be, as M. Rudler suggests, that this first sketch represented Adolphe as torn between the love of two women, Ellénore and a less worthy person of the type of Mrs. Trevor. He abandons Ellénore for the coquette; Ellénore dies of a broken heart and Adolphe refuses to see Mrs. Trevor again. It may well have been this first draft to which Madame de Stael refers in her letter to Bonstetten. We know from the *Journal Intime* that Constant realized thereafter that if a second woman were introduced into the novel, Ellénore would lose her central position and the weakness of Adolphe himself would become too odious. In the first fortnight of January 1807 he therefore rewrote the novel, more or less in its present form, and finished it within fifteen days. He read it aloud on repeated occasions and in different circles; the final draft was not written out until 1810; the novel was not printed until 1816. Two manuscript copies exist, the one in the library at Geneva, the other in the Monamy-Valin archives.

To us Anglo-Saxons, with our congenital reticence in all such matters, it may seem strange that Benjamin Constant should so frequently have indulged in the exhibitionism of reading aloud to strangers the story of his own amours. There was an element in his sensibility which added relish to such self-humiliation. He would have called it an act of conscience. There exist several records of these public readings. On 19 April 1815, we learn from the memoirs of the Duc de Broglie, Constant was feeling weary and exhausted; when he came to the death of Ellénore his voice broke; the whole audience dissolved into tears; and then as a reaction everybody started to laugh wildly. Constant notes this incident in his diary: *'Lu mon roman: fou rire.'* A few weeks later, on 20 June 1815, he went to the Rue Cerutti to read the novel to Queen Hortense. Before they had reached the death of Ellénore, the Duke of Rovigo entered the room hurriedly and took the Queen aside. He told her that Napoleon had been decisively defeated within a few miles of Brussels. The following February Miss Berry, in her journal, mentions a similar reading in London:

'Wednesday, February 14, 1816. In the evening at the Bourkes (the Danish Minister), where there had been a dinner. Lady Holland, Madame de Lieven etc., and where Benjamin Constant read his romance, or history; I do not know what to call it as he has not given it a name. It is very well written:—a sad, and much too true, history of the human heart; but almost ridiculously so, with the company before whom it was read. It lasted two hours and a half. The end was so touching that it was scarcely possible to restrain one's tears and the effort I made to do so made me positively ill. Agnes and I both burst into tears on our return home.'

The fame of these readings spread through London society. Constant decided to have the novel published. It was issued in French under the title *'Adolphe; an anecdote found among the papers of an unknown person and published by Monsieur Benjamin de Constant'*. It bears the double imprint of 'London, Colburn, Bookseller' and 'Paris, Tröttel and Wurtz'. On 17 August 1816, Constant wrote to his cousin from London: 'I only published the thing in order to save myself the trouble of reading it in company. Having given four readings in a single week, I thought it would be more worth while to allow others to have the trouble of reading it themselves.' Moreover, he received from Messrs. Colburn a welcome advance payment of £70. A second edition, with a new preface, was published in Paris a few weeks later. A third edition, with yet another preface, was published by Brissot-Thivers in Paris in 1824. The last edition to be published in Constant's lifetime appeared in 1828.

v

I HAVE BROUGHT the story of Benjamin Constant's loves and servitude up to that fortnight in January 1807 when he composed the basic draft of *Adolphe*. Before I examine how far the novel must be regarded as autobiographical, it may be well to sketch the outlines of Constant's subsequent career.

When in Germany in 1793, he had had an affair with Charlotte von Hardenberg which lasted for two months. He found her 'romantic and tiresome', and he went his way. At the time she made no attempt to recapture his affections; he discovered, characteristically, 'that something that escapes one is wholly different from something that pursues one'. Often, when lacerated by the claws of Madame de Stael, he had thought back upon Charlotte's gentle pliancy, her soothing hands. In 1807, when his hatred of Madame de Stael had reached its aching climax, he entered into correspondence with Charlotte who in the interval had married a Monsieur Dutertre. He asked her to obtain a divorce and to become his wife. Pliant, as usual, she travelled to Germany in order to institute divorce proceedings against the unfortunate Monsieur Dutertre. Constant had not, of course, dared to reveal these stratagems to Madame de Stael; in fact, to ease his conscience, he again begged her to become his wife. A scene followed in which she accused him, in front of her children, of seeking either to obtain her fortune or to destroy her life. As usual, he capitulated and returned submissively to Coppet. The old relations were resumed.

Meanwhile Charlotte had obtained her divorce from Monsieur Dutertre, and was expecting Benjamin to make the next move. At that very moment Madame de Stael went on a journey to Austria where she found a new lover in the shape of Maurice O'Donnell. Benjamin quickly seized this opportunity for escape. He married Charlotte at Brévans on 5 June 1808. Madame de Stael returned from Austria, having tired of O'Donnell, and re-established her court at Coppet. Benjamin did not dare to disclose to her his secret marriage: he remained at Coppet for almost a year, during which his only encounter with Charlotte was one frightened conversation conducted through the railings of the park. After months of further servitude he at last came to a decision. Charlotte herself must reveal to Madame de Stael the guilty secret which was theirs. The scene that followed had all the swift intensity of a typhoon. Madame de Stael imposed unconditional surrender. The marriage must remain a secret: Charlotte must disappear; and Benjamin must return to Coppet as if nothing had occurred. Charlotte thereupon attempted to commit suicide but recovered within a few days; and Benjamin remained a prisoner at Coppet until February 1811. It was then that John Rocca, a cavalry captain of the age of twenty-three, appeared as the deliverer. He was passionate and handsome; he was violent; he was sensual; he was a romantic and male. Moreover, he was not a conversationalist. 'Speech', admitted Madame de Stael, 'is not his language.' He challenged Benjamin to a duel because he objected to the attentions which he paid to Madame de Stael. The latter stopped the duel, but was entranced by the episode. At last Benjamin plucked up his courage. The final scene, and it was extravagant, took place on the staircase of the Hôtel de la Couronne at Lausanne at 11 A.M. on the morning of 10 May 1811. The chain at last was broken. Constant retired to Göttingen with Charlotte, where he settled down to a life of domestic austerity, studiously working at the twelve volumes of his *History of Religion*.

Then came Leipzig and the collapse of the Napoleonic Empire. The time for action had at last arrived. Constant, impulsive as ever, was whirled off his feet by a wind of political opportunism. He established relations with Bernadotte who, he imagined, was the most likely candidate for the Napoleonic succession. He went to Paris. By then Louis XVIII was established on the throne of his fathers and Constant, having rapidly severed his connection with Bernadotte, rallied to the Bourbon régime. When Napoleon landed at Fréjus, Constant publicly announced that he was prepared to sacrifice his life in order to repel the usurper and the tyrant; even when Napoleon had reached Auxerre, and Louis XVIII was preparing his escape to Ghent, Constant published in the *Journal des Débats* a wild manifesto of defiance. This juvenile conduct may have been due to his desire to impress Madame Récamier, with whom, since August 1814, he had fallen desperately in love. In the old Coppet days, Constant had scarcely noticed Juliette Récamier; 'not a single wrinkle,' he had written of her, 'not a single idea'; but by 1814 Madame Récamier was approaching her fortieth year, and Constant, who liked his fruit to be slightly over-ripe, entered upon the most unsuccessful, and therefore the most lasting, of his many love-affairs.

When Napoleon entered Paris, Constant escaped to the country where he remained for a few weeks in hiding. Having been assured that his life was in no danger, he crept back to Paris. Napoleon, realizing that the enthusiasm which had greeted his return could not be of long duration, was by then seeking to pose as a liberal. He sent for Benjamin Constant, appointed him a Councillor of State, and charged him with drafting the 'Additional Act to the Imperial Constitution'. When Napoleon returned from Waterloo he accorded Constant an audience of three hours which took place in the gardens of the Elysée. But the allies by then were advancing inexorably on Paris: Napoleon retired to Malmaison and thereafter to St. Helena; and Constant made his escape to London.

Having changed sides three times within one year, Constant then prepared to change sides once again. He had always believed that principles were more than parties; and it must be accorded to him in justice that, whatever may have been the colour of the successive cockades which in those breathless months he affixed to his buttonhole, he always remained a liberal at heart. He therefore made his peace with the Bourbons and returned to France. In 1819 he was elected for the Department of the Sarthe and, owing to a succession of trenchant speeches and pamphlets, became the acknowledged leader of the liberal opposition to the royalist reactionaries. He was unseated in 1822, but thereafter was elected for the Department of the Vosges amid scenes of popular rejoicing. With the Revolution of July it seemed that the road was at last opened to him for high office. But Louis Philippe, who was too shrewd a man not to realize Constant's inherent instability, merely accorded him the honorary post of President of the Council of State. Having failed as a politician, he endeavoured to confirm his reputation as a writer. In the autumn of 1830 he sought admission to the French Academy; he was not elected. On 10 December 1830 he died a disappointed man. His funeral acquired the proportions of a popular demonstration. But by posterity he is remembered, not as the author of the *History of Religion,* not as the able parliamentarian and the champion of liberalism, but as the man who, in that January fortnight of 1807, wrote the story of *Adolphe.*

VI

BENJAMIN CONSTANT adopted many devices in the hope of concealing from the public the fact that his novel was a record of personal experience. He pretended that the manuscript had come into his hands by chance, having been left behind by an unknown traveller in a Calabrian tavern. In the preface to the second edition he states expressly that 'none of the characters in *Adolphe* bears any relation to any person that I have ever known'. To identify the characters in the novel with any single individual was to indulge in 'a form of malignity which, aspiring to the merit of penetration, discovers allusions which are in fact based upon absurd conjectures'. He claimed that his novel had been written with a moral purpose; that it was a cautionary tale, devised to warn young men that it is a mistake to suppose that 'one can easily break attachments which one has formed lightheartedly'. In the third edition of 1824 he adopted an even more specious device. He contended that *Adolphe* was no more than a literary exercise, written with the sole idea of convincing several friends, who were staying together in the country, that it would be feasible to give some sort of interest to a story in which the characters would be restricted to two, and in which the situation would always remain the same'.

In private conversation, Constant was less obscurantist. We find the following in Samuel Rogers' diary for 14 July 1816: 'Benjamin Constant to breakfast. . . . *Adolphe,* many parts, he will confess, from his own experience. He had often in his mind an Englishwoman, —still living with a Frenchman in Paris—a Mrs. Lindsay.'

It is quite evident that the external circumstances, the factual apparatus, of the story were based—and deliberately based—upon the affair between Constant and Anna Lindsay. Ellénore was Polish by origin and Anna Irish; to the French mind in the early nineteenth century these two oppressed nationalities were analogous. The relations between Ellénore and the Comte de P—— are identical with those which had for so long existed between Anna Lindsay and Auguste de Lamoignon. The connection in each case had lasted for some twelve years and had acquired a tone of domestic respectability; two children had been born; and Ellénore had remained faithful to the Comte de P——, even as Anna Lindsay had remained faithful to Lamoignon, during the hard days of poverty and exile. Ellénore, like Anna, 'attached the greatest importance to regularity of conduct, precisely because hers was not regular according to conventional notions'. Even the minor characters—Juste de Constant, Madame de Charrière and Julie Talma—can readily be identified. In fact, the only fictional character in the whole novel is the Baron de T—— who would seem to be an idealization of Benjamin's father, in his more reflective moods.

There can be little doubt that Constant adopted this factual framework in order that Madame de Stael could at least pretend that the whole story was about someone else. If any awful doubt assailed her, she could always point to the key-sentence which Constant had introduced into Chapter II. 'Ellénore', he had written, 'was not a woman of exceptional intelligence.' Obviously, such a phrase could not, by any stretch of malignity, be applied to Germaine de Stael. She adopted the only attitude which was open to her to adopt; she accepted the story at its face value, and she pressed it upon her friends as a remarkable account of an episode which had occurred when Benjamin was on leave. 'The first time I ever read it', wrote Byron in sending the book to Lady Blessington, 'was at the desire of Madame de Stael, who was supposed by the good-natured world to be the heroine . . . which she was not, and was furious at the supposition.'

Madame de Stael possessed, it is true, unlimited powers of self-deception: with a sweep of the wing she could hurl any unwanted fledgeling from the cluttered bird's-nest of her mind. Yet it is difficult to believe that when she read and re-read the pages of *Adolphe* some suspicion did not occur to her that here, transparently disguised, was a tortured protest and an agonized appeal.

There were in the first place certain events, certain circumstances, certain psychological states, which could not possibly apply to the Benjamin-Anna relation and which certainly applied to the Benjamin-de Stael relation. There was the death of M. Necker; there was Madame de Stael's expulsion by Napoleon's police; there was the financial obligation into which Benjamin had entered both to M. Necker and to Germaine herself, and which envenomed his dependence. She must have realized that the affair between Benjamin and Anna had not lasted quite long enough to produce that sense of intimacy, that deep familiarity, which could justify the words 'We were living on the memories of our hearts'. She must have known that when he wrote of Caden he was thinking of Coppet. She was too intelligent a woman not to see that the 'destructive passion', the actual rage and violence, manifested by Ellénore were inconsistent with her comparatively placid character, or that the reckless indiscretion which she displayed was out of harmony with her prim and calculating nature. Some fibre of self-reproach must surely have been set vibrating in Madame de Stael's egoism when she read the phrase 'I recognized in Ellénore the denial of all the success to which I might have aspired'. She must have known that when he wrote of this inexorable chain, this horrible incarceration, this 'fantastic despotism', he was not really thinking of Anna Lindsay but of the ruthless tyranny which she herself had exercised for all those years. And it must have been with anguish—or was it only with seething rage?—that her eyes lighted upon the implied but piteous appeal: 'What have I not sacrificed for Ellénore? For her sake I left my home and family; for her sake I am living in this place, where my youth slips away in solitude, without glory, without honour, and without delight. . . . Yet it is time that I embarked on a career, began a life of action, acquired some claim to the esteem of my fellow men and put my faculties to some worthy use.' This supposition must have occurred to her; she may perhaps, as Byron said, have thereby been rendered 'furious'; I hope she was also rendered ashamed.

It is useless to pretend that the character of Benjamin Constant as he portrays it in the pages of *Adolphe* is an estimable character. He was an intelligent but unattractive man. 'He does not manage even', wrote Pauline de Beaumont to Joubert, 'to like himself.' 'I possess excellent qualities', confessed Constant to his diary, 'such as pride, generosity and devotion, but I am not quite a real person.' M. du Bos denies the latter accusation. 'Never', he writes, 'has any man been more authentic.' There was, as so many have recognized, a dualism in Constant's character which enabled him to observe with lucidity and detachment the vagaries and the results of his own actions. And perhaps his vanity, his ruthlessness, and his appalling weakness are redeemed by the fact that he possessed an unlimited fund of human pity; he suffered atrociously—as Byron did not suffer—from the pain which he caused.

It may be interesting, in conclusion, to refer to the effect produced by *Adolphe* upon successive generations. Constant's contemporaries and compatriots, versed as they were in the doctrine of 'sensibility', trained as they had been in the self-expository novel by *René* and *Corinne,* and even Madame de Krüdener's *Valérie,* found in it a highly romantic exposition of the conflict between personal emotion and the social conventions. Yet even in 1816 Byron (who had some knowledge of similar situations) remarked that 'it leaves an unpleasant impression'. Succeeding generations, fortified as they were by moral earnestness, regarded *Adolphe* as ethically and artistically abhorrent; as M. Fabre-Luce has noted, Sismondi, who had been swept off his feet by *Adolphe* in 1816, found it detestable when he re-read it in 1837. Between 1840 and 1870 *Adolphe* was repudiated and ignored. With the revival of individualism in the early eighties, with the spread of the analytical spirit, it was suddenly discovered that *Adolphe* possessed the unique virtue of 'sincerity'. 'People used to find fault with Adolphe', wrote Anatole France, 'but now we pity him.' For Paul Bourget, Constant was a man who despised hypocrisy and who became virtuous through self-revelation; Barrès saw in him the intellectual, toying with his own sensations; for him Constant became the 'Great Saint' of the *culte de moi*. And what of today? The present generation can read *Adolphe* with interest, partly because of its importance in the development of the French analytical novel, partly because of the excellence of its style and the subtlety of its interpretation of character, and partly because it describes what actually happens in life, rather than what ought ideally to occur. It responds to the realism of our present age, to our dislike of all synthetic formulas, and to the sad fatalism which leads so many young people to imagine that the fortunes of men are determined, not by their strength or virtues, but by their weakness and their faults.

HAROLD NICOLSON

ADOLPHE

TRANSLATED FROM THE FRENCH

BY

CARL WILDMAN

Author's Preface to the Third Edition
1824

IT WAS NOT WITHOUT some hesitation that I agreed to the reprinting of this little work, published ten years ago. But for the fact that I was almost certain that a pirated edition would appear in Belgium and that, like the majority of the pirated editions which the Belgian publishers distribute in Germany and introduce into France, it would contain additions and interpolations for which I was not responsible, I should never have bothered about this anecdote. I wrote it with the sole idea of convincing several friends, who were staying together in the country, that it was feasible to give some sort of interest to a story in which the characters would be restricted to two, and in which the situation would always remain the same.

When I had started on this work, I wanted to develop several ideas which occurred to me and seemed to me not uninstructive. I wanted to depict the harm which is done even to barren hearts by the suffering they themselves cause to others, and the illusion which makes them believe themselves more frivolous and corrupt than they really are. From a distance, the pain you inflict appears confused and vague, like a cloud through which you could easily pass; you are encouraged by an approving and artificial society which substitutes rules for principles, conventions for emotions, and which hates scandal because it is a nuisance—not because it is immoral. It accepts vice quite happily when there is no scandal. You imagine that attachments which you form lightheartedly can be broken easily. But when you see the anguish caused by these broken bonds, the pain and astonishment of a deluded soul, the esteem which is repressed and which finds no outlet, the mistrust which replaces so complete a confidence and which, inevitably directed against the loved one, spreads to the whole world, then it is you realize that there is something sacred in a heart which suffers because it loves. You discover how deep are the roots of the affection you thought you inspired but did not share; and if you overcome what you call weakness, you do so only by destroying in your character all that is generous, faithful, noble and kind. You rise from this victory, which other people and friends applaud, having killed part of your soul, set sympathy at nought, taken advantage of weakness, outraged morality whilst using it as an excuse for harshness, and, ashamed or perverted by this success, you outlive your better nature.

That was what I tried to portray in *Adolphe*. I do not know if I have succeeded; but one thing makes me feel *Adolphe* has the merit of possessing a measure of truth: almost all my readers whom I have met have told me that they themselves have been in the same position as my hero. It is true that, while expressing regrets at having caused all that pain, they could not wholly conceal a fatuous self-satisfaction. They were pleased to depict themselves as having, like Adolphe, been the prey of the stubborn affections which they had inspired and the victims of the immense love conceived for them. I believe that, on the whole, they were calumniating themselves and that, had their vanity left them in peace, their conscience could have remained at rest.

Be that as it may, *Adolphe* has become a matter of complete indifference to me; I attach no importance to this novel and, I repeat, my sole object in letting it reappear for the benefit of a public who have probably forgotten it, if they ever knew it, is to declare that any edition containing anything not in this edition is not by me and I cannot be held responsible for it.[1]

---

[1] The translator, nevertheless, has thought fit to revert to the text of the earlier editions in one small detail, i.e. in the first sentence of Chapter IX he has substituted 'first' for 'last'—'last' appearing to be an unfortunate correction, probably on the part of the author.

C.W.

Publisher's Foreword

SOME YEARS AGO, I was travelling through Italy. The flooding of the Neto forced me to stop at Cerenza and put up at one of the inns in this little village in Calabria; at the same inn was a stranger who had been obliged to stay there for the same reason. He was very silent and appeared sad: he showed no impatience. Occasionally, as he was the only person in that part with whom I could talk, I complained to him about this hindrance to our journey. 'Wherever I am', he replied, 'makes no difference to me.' Our host, who had chatted with a Neapolitan who served this man without knowing his name, told me that this person was not travelling out of curiosity, for he visited no ruins, nor historic sites, nor monuments, nor men. He read much, but only by fits and starts; he went for a walk every evening, always alone, and he often spent whole days sitting motionless with his head resting on his two hands.

Just when the roads were reopened and we could have set out, this stranger fell very ill. Common humanity made it my duty to extend my stay in order to look after him. At Cerenza, there was only a village surgeon, and I wanted to send to Cosenza for more effective aid. 'Do not bother,' said the stranger, 'the village surgeon is just what I need.' He was right, though perhaps in a way he had not meant, for this man cured him. 'I had no idea you were so clever,' he said to him with a certain ill-humour as he dismissed him; then he thanked me for my kindness and left.

Several months later, in Naples, I received a letter from our host of Cerenza with a casket found on the road leading to Strongoli, the road which the stranger and myself had followed, but separately. The innkeeper who sent it to me was convinced it belonged to one of us.

It contained many very old letters, without addresses, or from which the addresses and signatures had been erased, the portrait of a woman and a notebook containing the anecdote or account we are about to read. When saying farewell, the stranger to whom these effects belonged left me no means of communicating with him. Not being sure what I should do with these documents, I kept them for ten years, and, having one day by chance mentioned them to a few people in a German town, one of these persons pressed me to entrust him with the manuscript in my possession. A week later, the manuscript was returned to me with a letter I have put at the end of this story because it would be unintelligible if you read it before being acquainted with the story itself.

This letter decided me to make the present publication, for it made quite clear that publication could neither offend nor compromise anyone. I have not changed a word of the original; even the suppression of proper names is not my doing: in the manuscript they were designated, as they still are, by initial letters.

I I WAS TWENTY-TWO AND HAD JUST FINISHED MY
studies at the University of Göttingen. My
father, a minister of the Elector of ——, intended me to visit the most interesting countries of Europe, and then enter, at his side, the department of which he was the head, in order to prepare
me for the day on which I should take his place.
Though leading a dissipated life, I had worked rather
doggedly and achieved some successes which distinguished me from my fellow students and caused my
father to entertain hopes concerning my future which
were probably much exaggerated.

These high hopes made him usually very lenient with
me when I committed indiscretions. He never let me
suffer from the consequences of my misconduct; in fact,
he always granted and sometimes anticipated my requests in these matters.

Unfortunately, his attitude was noble and generous
rather than tender. I was deeply conscious of his right
to my gratitude and respect; but no confidence had
ever existed between us. There was something ironical
in his mentality which agreed ill with my character.
My sole desire at that time was to give myself up to
those primitive and passionate feelings which throw
the mind out of harmony with the ordinary world and
inspire contempt for all about one. In my father I found
not a critic, but a cold and caustic observer who began
by smiling out of pity but soon showed impatience to
end the conversation. I do not remember in my first
eighteen years ever having had an hour's conversation
with him. His letters were affectionate, full of reasonable and considerate advice; but hardly were we to-

gether than he showed a constraint which I could not
explain and which caused a painful reaction in me. I
did not then know what timidity meant—that inner
suffering which pursues you into old age, which forces
the profoundest feelings back into the heart, chilling
your words and deforming in your mouth whatever
you try to say, allowing you to express yourself only in
vague phrases or a somewhat bitter irony, as if you
wanted to avenge yourself on your feelings for the
pain you experienced at being unable to communicate
them. I did not know that my father was timid, even
with his son, and that often, having waited a long
while for some sign of affection from me which his
apparent coldness seemed to prohibit, he would leave
me, his eyes moist with tears, and complain to others
that I did not love him.

My feeling of constraint with him had a great influence on my character. I was as timid as he, but, being
younger, I was more excitable. I kept to myself all that
I felt, made all my plans on my own, and relied on myself to put them into effect. I considered the opinion,
interest, assistance and even the mere presence of
others as a hindrance and an obstacle. I developed the
habit of never speaking of what I was doing, of endur-
ing conversation only as a tiresome necessity, and then
enlivening it by perpetual joking which made it less
wearisome to me, and helped to hide my real thoughts.
Hence a certain reserve with which my friends reproach me even today, and a difficulty in conversing
seriously which I still find hard to overcome. From the
same cause sprang an ardent desire for independence,
a considerable impatience with all ties and an invinci-
ble terror at forming new ones. I felt at ease only when
quite alone, and such, even now, is the effect of this
disposition that in the most trifling circumstances,
when I have to choose between two courses of action,
a human face disturbs me and my natural impulse is to
flee in order to deliberate in peace.

However, I did not possess the depths of egoism
which such a character would seem to indicate. Though
only interested in myself, I was but faintly interested.
Unconsciously I bore in my heart a need for sympathy

which, not being satisfied, caused me to abandon, one after another, every object of my curiosity. This indifference to everything was further strengthened by the idea of death, an idea which had impressed itself upon me when I was very young. I have never been able to understand how men could so readily cease to be fully alive to this notion. At the age of seventeen, I saw a woman die whose strange and remarkable cast of mind had begun to develop my mind. This woman, like so many others, had at the outset plunged into social life, of which she was ignorant, with the feeling that she possessed great strength of character and really powerful faculties. As with so many others, also, her hopes were disappointed because she did not bow to arbitrary but necessary conventions; her youth passed without pleasure and, finally, old age overtook her without subduing her. She lived in a country house, neighboring on one of our estates, dissatisfied and solitary, her only resource her mind with which she analysed everything. For nearly a year, during our inexhaustible conversations, we considered life in all its aspects and death always as the end of all things; and, after I had so often discussed death with her, death struck her down before my eyes.

This incident filled me with a feeling of uncertainty concerning fate and a vague dreaminess which never left me. In the poets, I read for preference whatever recalled the brevity of human life. I felt that no object was worth an effort. Is is rather curious that this feeling has weakened as the weight of years has increased. Could it be that there is something dubious about hope and that when hope has disappeared from a man's life his life assumes a more severe and positive character? Could it be that life seems so much the more real when all illusions have vanished, just as the contours of a mountain ridge appear more clearly on the horizon when the clouds are gone?

On leaving Göttingen, I went to the little town of D——. This town was the residence of a Prince who, like most of the princes of Germany, ruled in benign fashion over a State of small area, protecting enlightened men who came to settle there, and allowing complete

freedom to all opinions; but having been restricted
by ancient custom to the society of courtiers, he assembled about him, for that same reason, only men
who were on the whole insignificant and mediocre. I
was welcomed into that court with the curiosity which
any stranger would naturally inspire who could break
the circle of monotony and etiquette. For several
months I perceived nothing which could hold my attention. I was grateful for the kindness I was shown,
but either my timidity prevented me from enjoying it
or, rather than tire myself with aimless excitement, I
preferred solitude to the insipid pleasures in which I
was invited to take part.

I had no strong dislike for anyone, but few people
aroused my interest; now, men take offence at indifference; they attribute it to ill-will or to affectation;
they will not believe that it is natural for one to
find their company wearisome. Sometimes, I tried to
master my boredom; I took refuge in deep silence. At
other times, tiring of my own silence, I indulged in a
few jokes, and once my mind had been stimulated in
this direction it carried me away until I exceeded all
bounds. In the course of a single day I would unveil
all the ridiculous traits of character which I had observed during a month. Those to whom I confided my
sudden and involuntary outpourings were not grateful
to me and in that they were right; for it was not the
need to confide but the need to talk which had possessed me.

I had contracted, in my conversations with the
woman who had first developed my ideas, an insurmountable aversion to all truisms and dogmatic sayings. Therefore, when I heard mediocrities holding forth
with complacency on firmly established and undeniable
principles of morality, behavior or religion—things
which they are only too apt to place on the same level—
I felt obliged to contradict them; not that I had
adopted contrary opinions but because I was irritated
by so firm and weighty a conviction. Moreover, some
vague instinct put me on my guard against these truisms, so sweeping and free from any fine distinctions.
Foolish people make one compact and indivisible

block of their morality, so that it interferes only to the slightest degree with their actions and leaves them complete freedom in all details.

I soon acquired, through this behaviour, a great reputation for insincerity, a bantering wit and maliciousness. My bitter words were considered proof of my spiteful mind, my jokes outrages against all that was most worthy of respect. Those whom I had made the mistake of ridiculing found it convenient to make common cause with the principles they accused me of calling into question. Since I had unwittingly made them laugh at each other, they all joined forces against me. It was as if, in bringing their ridiculous traits of character to their notice, I had betrayed a confidence; or as if, in revealing themselves to me as they were, they had extracted a promise of silence from me. I, for one, was unaware of having agreed to such an onerous pact. They had enjoyed allowing themselves free scope; I had enjoyed observing and describing them; and what they called perfidy seemed to me a very legitimate and quite innocent compensation.

I am not seeking hereby to justify myself. That frivolous and facile habit of an immature mind was renounced by me a long while ago. I simply wish to state for the benefit of others, since I have now retired from the world, that it takes time to accustom one's self to mankind, fashioned as it is by self-interest, affectation, vanity and fear. The astonishment of youth at the appearance of so artificial and laboured a society denotes an unspoiled heart rather than a malicious mind. Moreover, society has nothing to fear on that account. It weighs so heavily upon us, its blind influence is so powerful, that it soon shapes us in the universal mould. We are then merely surprised at our first astonishment, and we feel happy in our new shape, just as one finally manages to breathe freely in a congested theatre, whereas, on first entering, one breathed with difficulty.

If some escape from this general fate, they repress their secret dissent; they perceive in most ridiculous traits of character the seed of vices; they do not joke at them because contempt replaces mockery and contempt is silent.

A vague uneasiness concerning my character therefore grew in my immediate social circle. No blameworthy action could be cited against me; and, further, some actions which seemed to indicate generosity or devotion could not be contested; but they said I was immoral and untrustworthy—two epithets which, fortunately for them, were invented to enable such people to insinuate facts of which they have no cognizance and to suggest whatever they do not know.

II BEING DREAMY, INATTENTIVE AND BORED, I WAS not aware of the impression I was producing. I was devoting my time to frequently interrupted studies, to plans which I did not put into execution and to half-hearted pleasures, when a circumstance which seemed, on the face of it, very frivolous, produced a great revolution in my disposition.

A young man, with whom I was on fairly intimate terms, had been trying for some months to attract one of the less insipid women who frequented the circle in which we moved; he confided in me, as in a thoroughly impartial person, the progress of his venture. After prolonged efforts he managed to win her love; and, as he had not hidden his reverses and his disappointments from me, he felt obliged to tell me of his successes: his rapture and great joy had no equal. The spectacle of such happiness made me regret not having as yet attempted the like; until that time I had had no liaison with a woman of a sort to satisfy my self-esteem; a new horizon seemed to open before my eyes; I became conscious of a new need at the bottom of my heart. There was, no doubt, much vanity in this need, but not vanity alone; there was perhaps less vanity than I myself believed. Men's feelings are

obscure and confused; they are composed of a great
number and variety of impressions which defy observa-
tion; and words, always too crude and too general,
may well indicate them but can never define them.

In my father's house I had adopted, in regard to
women, a rather immoral attitude. Although my father
strictly observed the proprieties, he frequently indulged in frivolous remarks concerning affairs of the
heart: he looked on them as excusable if not permis-
sible amusements, and considered nothing in a serious
light, save marriage. His one principle was that a
young man must studiously avoid what is called an
act of folly, that is to say, contracting a lasting en-
gagement with a person who is not absolutely his
equal in regard to fortune, birth and outward advantages; he saw no objection—provided there was no
question of marriage—to taking any woman and then
leaving her; and I have seen him smile with a sort of
approbation at this parody of a well-known saying:
It hurts them so little and gives us so much pleasure!

It is not sufficiently realized how deep an impression can be made in early youth by sayings of this sort,
and to what extent, at an age when every opinion appears dubious and unsettled, children are amazed at
finding the clear rules they have been taught contradicted by jokes which win general applause. In their
eyes those rules cease to be anything but banal pre-
cepts which their parents have agreed upon and which
they repeat to children out of a mere sense of duty,
whilst the jokes appear to hold the real key to life.

Some obscure emotion agitated me. I want to be
loved, I thought to myself; and I looked around me
but could see no one who inspired love in me, no one
likely to want love. I examined my heart and my tastes; I
could find no marked preference. I was in this restless
state of mind, when I made the acquaintance of Count
P——, a man aged forty, whose family was related to
mine. He suggested my going to see him. It was an ill-
fated visit. Living with him was his mistress, a Polish
woman who was celebrated for her beauty, although
no longer in her first youth.

Despite the difficulties of her situation, this woman

had on several occasions shown the distinction of her
character. She came of a rather famous Polish family,
which had been ruined in the troubles that beset her
country. Her father had been banished, her mother
took refuge in France and brought her daughter with
her. At her death, the daughter was left completely on
her own. Count P—— fell in love with her. I never knew
how this liaison arose. When I first saw Ellénore, it
had existed for some time and had been, as it were,
sanctioned. It may have been the inevitable outcome
of her situation, or due to the inexperience of her
age, that she launched on a career which was repugnant
to her by her education and her habits and by the
pride which formed so notable a part of her character.
All I know, and all anybody knew, is that, when Count
P—— was almost entirely ruined and his liberty threatened, Ellénore gave him such proofs of devotion, rejected with such scorn the most brilliant offers, shared
his risks and his poverty with such enthusiasm and, in
fact, joy, that even with the most severe scruples one
could not but render justice to the purity of her motives
and the disinterestedness of her conduct. It was to her
activity, to her courage, to her good sense, to her sacrifices of every kind which she supported without complaint, that her lover owed the recovery of a part of
his property. They had come to settle in D—— in order
to follow a lawsuit which might allow Count P—— to
recover all his former wealth, and they expected to
stay there about two years.

Ellénore was not a woman of exceptional intelligence; but her ideas were sound and her way of expressing them, which was always simple, was sometimes
made striking by the nobility and loftiness of her sentiments. She had many prejudices; but all of them ran
counter to her interest. She attached the greatest importance to regularity of conduct, precisely because
hers was not regular according to conventional notions.
She was very religious, because religion severely condemned her kind of life. In conversation, she shunned
anything which, to other women, would merely appear
innocent jokes, because she was always afraid that
someone might, as a result, imagine that remarks in

bad taste could be addressed to her on account of her position. She would have preferred only to receive people of the highest rank and of irreproachable morals, because the women with whom she feared to be compared generally form a mixed class and, having resigned themselves to the loss of consideration, merely seek amusement in society.

In a word, Ellénore was for ever struggling against her destiny. All her deeds and words formed a protest against the class in which she found herself; and, as she felt that reality was stronger than she and that her efforts altered her situation not a little, she was very unhappy. She raised the two children she had had by Count P—— in an exceedingly austere fashion. It appeared sometimes as though they were in a way a nuisance to her, and a secret revolt mingled with the passionate rather than tender attachment which she showed for them. When any well-intentioned remark was made about the children growing up or about the promise of talents they showed, or the careers they would make, she would pale at the thought that one day she would have to tell them the facts of their birth. But at the slightest danger, or after an hour's absence, she would return to them with an anxiety in which one could detect a kind of remorse and the desire to give them through her caresses the happiness which was denied to her.

This opposition between her sentiments and her position in society caused her to be most changeable in mood. She was often dreamy and taciturn; sometimes she spoke in impetuous fashion. As a single idea preoccupied her, she never remained perfectly calm, even in the midst of the most general conversation. For this very reason there was something spirited and unexpected in her manner which made her more striking than she would have been naturally. The strangeness of her position made up for the lack of novelty in her ideas. One observed her with interest and curiosity, like a magnificent thunderstorm.

Coming into my ken at a time when my heart needed love and my vanity success, Ellénore seemed to me a worthy conquest. She herself found some pleasure in the society of a man who was different from those she had seen till then. Her circle consisted of a few friends and relations of her lover and their wives who, because of the great influence of Count P——, had been obliged to receive his mistress. The husbands had as few feelings as they had ideas. The wives differed from their husbands only in that their mediocrity was of a more anxious and restless variety. They did not possess the calm of mind which comes from an occupation and the regularity it entails. A lighter-hearted and more varied conversation, a peculiar mixture of melancholy and gaiety, of discouragement and interest, of enthusiasm and irony, astonished and delighted Ellénore. She spoke several languages, imperfectly it is true, but always with vivacity and sometimes with grace. Her ideas seemed to become clearer because of the difficulties she experienced and even to emerge from the struggle more pleasing, fresh and artless; for foreign idioms rejuvenate thoughts and free them from the turns of speech which make them appear either commonplace or affected. We read English poetry together; we went for walks together. I often paid her a visit in the morning and again in the evening. I talked on a great many subjects with her.

I thought I was going to size up her character and mind as a cool and impartial observer; but every word she spoke to me seemed to possess an inexplicable grace. My intention to attract her introduced a new interest into my life and enlivened my existence to an unaccustomed extent. I attributed this magical effect to her charm; I should have enjoyed it still more completely but for the vow to do honour to my self-esteem. That self-esteem stood between Ellénore and myself. I fancied I was obliged to make for the intended goal by the quickest road: I did not therefore give myself up unreservedly to my impressions. I was anxious to speak to her since I believed I had only to speak in order to succeed. I did not believe I loved Ellénore; but I could no longer entertain the idea of not pleasing her. All the while she occupied my thoughts. I made hundreds of plans; I invented hundreds of ways of effecting my conquest with that kind of fatuity due to inexperience which makes one feel sure of success because nothing has been essayed.

An unconquerable timidity, however, always stopped me; all my speeches died on my lips or ended in a very different way from that which I intended. A struggle went on within me; I was enraged with myself.

And I tried to find a rational explanation which would extricate me from the struggle undiminished in my own estimation. I told myself I should not be over-hasty as Ellénore was not prepared for the confession I was contemplating, and it would be better to wait longer. In order to live at peace with ourselves, we almost always disguise our impotence or weakness as calculated actions and systems, and so we satisfy that part of us which is observing the other.

This situation continued indefinitely. Each day I decided that the next was to be the absolute date for a positive declaration and each morrow passed like the eve. My timidity disappeared as soon as I left Ellénore; I then started afresh with my clever plans and deep-laid schemes; but scarcely was I with her again than I felt nervous and uneasy. If anyone could have read in my heart when I was away from her, he would have taken me for a cold and unfeeling seducer; if anyone could have seen me at her side, he would have taken me for a passionate but bewildered novice of a lover. Both these judgments would have been incorrect; there is no such thing as complete unity in man, and no one is ever completely sincere or completely insincere.

These repeated experiences convinced me that I should never have the courage to speak to Ellénore, and so I decided to write to her. Count P—— was away. The long inner conflict with my own character, the impatience I felt at being unable to dominate it, the uncertainty as to the success of my enterprise, filled my letter with an agitation which closely resembled love. Moreover, excited as I was by my own style, I felt, when finishing my letter, some of the passion which I had sought to express with all the conviction I could summon.

Ellénore saw in my letter what it was natural to

see; the emotion of a man ten years younger than herself whose heart was opening to sentiments as yet unknown to him, and who deserved pity rather than anger. She replied to me gently, gave me some kindly advice, offered me her sincere friendship, but told me that, until the return of Count P——, she could not receive me.

The reply came as a shock to me. My imagination, inflamed by this obstacle, took possession of my whole existence. The love which, an hour earlier, I had congratulated myself on feigning I now thought I felt with frenzy. I ran to Ellénore; I was told she was out. I wrote to her; I begged her to grant me a last interview; in heart-breaking terms I described my despair and the baleful projects which her cruel decision inspired in me. During the greater part of the day I vainly waited for a reply. The only way I could ease my unspeakable suffering was to persuade myself that, the next day I would brave all obstacles and force my way to Ellénore. I would speak to her! In the evening, I received a few words from her: they were gentle. I thought I could discern in them an impression of regret and sadness; but she persisted in her resolve which she said was unshakable. I went to her house again the next day. She had gone to a part of the country of which her servants did not know the name. They did not even know of any way of communicating my letters to her.

I stayed motionless at her door for a long while, imagining I should never have the opportunity of seeing her again. I myself was astonished at the depth of my suffering. In my mind, I went over again the time when I had affirmed that my only desire was to achieve a triumph, and had said that this was merely an adventure which I would have no difficulty in abandoning. I had had no idea of the violent, uncontrollable pain which was to tear my heart. Several days passed in this way. I was unable to find distraction or to study. I kept wandering in front of Ellénore's door. I walked about the town as though, at the corner of each street, I expected to meet her. One morning, during one of these aimless wanderings which served

to replace my agitation by fatigue, I saw the coach of
Count P—— who was returning from his journey. He
recognized me and dismounted. After a few banal remarks, disguising my emotion, I spoke to him of Ellénore's sudden departure. 'Yes,' he replied, 'one of
her women friends a good few miles from here, has
had some misfortune and Ellénore imagined her presence might be of assistance. She left without consulting me. She is a person who is dominated by her
heart. In self-sacrifice she almost finds repose for her
restless feelings. But her presence here is too necessary
for me; I shall write to her: she will certainly return
within a few days.'

This assurance calmed me; I felt my pain become
less acute. For the first time since Ellénore's departure,
I could breathe without difficulty. Her return was less
prompt than Count P—— had hoped. But I had resumed
my usual life and the anguish I had felt began to lessen when, after a month, Count P—— informed me that
Ellénore was to arrive that evening. As he set great
store on preserving the place in society which her
character deserved and from which her situation
seemed to exclude her, he invited to supper several
women friends and relations' wives who had consented
to see Ellénore.

My memories revived, at first confused then more
vivid. My self-esteem was implicated. I was embarrassed
and humiliated at the idea of meeting a woman who
had treated me like a child. I seemed to see her, when
I approached, smiling at the thought that a short absence had calmed the effervescence of a youthful head;
and I distinguished in that smile a sort of contempt.
By degrees, my feelings were revived. I had risen that
day without thought of Ellénore; yet an hour after
receiving news of her arrival, her image constantly
floated before my eyes, ruling my heart, and I had a
fever at the fear of not seeing her.

I stayed indoors all that day; I stayed, as it were,
hidden; I was in fear and trembling lest the slightest
movement on my part should forestall our meeting.
Yet nothing was simpler or more certain; but I desired
it with such fervour that it appeared impossible to me.

I was devoured by impatience. Every minute I looked at my watch. I was obliged to open the window to breathe; my blood was like fire circulating in my veins.

At last I heard the hour strike when I was to go to the Count's. My impatience was suddenly changed to timidity; I dressed myself slowly; I no longer felt in a hurry to arrive: I had such a fear that my hopes might be disappointed, such a keen presentiment of the pain I was in danger of experiencing, that I would willingly have agreed to defer everything.

It was fairly late when I made my way into Count P——'s house. I perceived Ellénore sitting at the other end of the room; I dared not advance as it seemed to me that everyone's eyes were fixed on me. I went and hid in a corner of the room, behind a group of men who were in conversation. From there, I comtemplated Ellénore: she appeared to be slightly changed, she was paler than usual. The Count discovered me in the kind of retreat where I had taken refuge; he came to me, took me by the hand and led me to Ellénore. 'May I introduce', he said, laughing, 'one of the men your unexpected departure most astonished.' Ellénore was talking to a woman sitting beside her. When she saw me, the words froze on her lips; she was utterly bewildered, and so to a great extent was I.

We could be overheard, and so I asked her some ordinary questions. We both resumed an appearance of calm. Supper was announced; I offered Ellénore my arm, which she could not refuse. 'If,' I said as I escorted her, 'if you will not promise to receive me tomorrow at eleven o'clock, I shall go away at once, I shall abandon my country, my family and my father, I shall break all my ties, I shall refuse to perform any of my duties, and I shall go, no matter where, to finish as quickly as possible a life which you take pleasure in poisoning.' 'Adolphe!' she cried, then hesitated. I made as if to go. I do not know what my face expressed, but I have never experienced so violent a contraction of the features.

Ellénore looked at me. Terror mingled with affection in her face. 'I will receive you tomorrow,' she said, 'but I implore you. . . .' A number of people were following us and she could not finish her sentence. I pressed her hand with my arm; we took our places at table.

I would have liked to sit beside Ellénore, but the master of the house had decided otherwise: I was placed almost opposite her. At the beginning of the supper, she was thoughtful. When she was spoken to, she replied softly; but she soon relapsed into her distracted state. One of her friends, struck by her silence and her dejection, asked her if she was unwell. 'My health has not been good lately,' she replied, 'and at the moment it is sadly impaired.' I was desirous of producing an agreeable impression on Ellénore; I wanted, by showing myself likeable and witty, to dispose her in my favour and prepare her for the interview she had granted me. I therefore tried in countless ways to fix her attention. I led the conversation round to subjects which I knew interested her; our neighbours took part; I was inspired by her presence; I managed to gain her attention and soon saw her smile: I felt such joy at this, my looks expressed so much gratitude, that she could not have failed to be moved. Her sadness and her distraction began to disappear: she no longer resisted the secret charm which invaded her mind at the sight of the happiness I owed to her; and when we left the table, perfect understanding reigned in our hearts as if we had never been separated. 'You see,' I said, as I gave her my hand to lead her to the drawing-room, 'you dispose of my whole life. What had I done that you should delight in making it a torment?'

III I SPENT A SLEEPLESS NIGHT. THERE WAS NO longer any question in my mind of schemes or plans; I was perfectly convinced that I was really in love. It was no longer the hope of success which impelled me to act: the need to see the person whom I loved and to enjoy her presence dominated me to the exclusion of all else. Eleven o'clock chimed and I went to Ellénore; she was waiting for me. She wished to speak: I asked her to listen. I sat beside her, for I could scarcely stand on my legs, and I continued in these words, not, however, without being frequently obliged to stop:

'I have not come to appeal against the sentence you have passed; nor have I come to retract a confession which may have offended you; I could not if I wanted to. The love which you shun cannot be destroyed: the very effort which I am making to speak with as much calm as I can summon is a proof of the violence of the feeling which wounds you. Nor is it in order to speak of this that I have asked you to listen to me; it is, on the contrary, to beg you to forget it and to receive me as formerly; to put out of your mind a momentary aberration and not to punish me because you know a secret which I should have kept locked in the depths of my soul. You know my situation, that character of mine which people call strange and unsociable, that heart which is out of tune with all the interests of others, which is solitary in the midst of society, yet which suffers from the solitude to which it is condemned. Your friendship gave me support: without that friendship I cannot live. I have become accustomed to seeing you; you have allowed that sweet habit to be formed: what have I done that I should lose that one and only consolation in so sad and dismal an existence? I am horribly unhappy; I no longer have the courage to bear such a protracted state of unhappiness; I hope for nothing. I ask for nothing, I only wish to see you: but see you I must if I am to live.'

Ellénore remained silent. 'What do you fear?' I continued. 'What am I asking of you? Only what you grant to all and sundry. Do you fear society? Society is absorbed in its own solemn frivolities and will not read in a heart like mine. How should I be anything but prudent? Is not my life at stake? Ellénore, yield to my prayer: you will find some sweetness in it. There will be some charm in being loved like this, in seeing me beside you, concerned only with you, existing solely for you, owing to you every pleasurable sensation to which I am still alive, and saved by your presence from suffering and despair.'

I continued a long time in this manner, countering all objections and presenting in a hundred different ways all the reasons which pleaded in my favour. I was so submissive, so resigned, I asked for so little, I should be so unhappy at a refusal!

Ellénore was touched. She imposed several conditions. She agreed to receive me but seldom, and then only in a numerous gathering, with the pledge that I would never speak of love. I promised what she required. We were both happy: I at having regained the possession I was in danger of losing, and Ellénore at finding that she could, at the same time, be generous, feeling and prudent.

The very next day I took advantage of the permission I had obtained; and continued so to do on the days following. Ellénore no longer saw the necessity for making my visits infrequent: soon, nothing seemed more natural to her than to see me every day. Ten years of fidelity had inspired in Count P—— an absolute confidence; he allowed Ellénore the greatest liberty. As he had had to fight against opinion which wanted to exclude his mistress from the society in which he lived, he liked to see her circle enlarged; a full house was a proof to him of his triumph over opinion.

When I used to arrive, I could see in Ellénore's looks an expression of pleasure. When she was amused in the course of conversation, she automatically turned her eyes to me. Nothing interesting was recounted without her calling me to hear it. But she was never alone: whole evenings passed without my being able to say anything more personal than a few insignificant or interrupted words. It was not long before I began to chafe at so much constraint. I became melancholy, taciturn, moody and bitter in my conversation. I could scarcely contain myself when another than I talked alone with Ellénore; I would abruptly break into these conversations. I cared little that people might take offence at this and I was not always stayed by the fear of compromising Ellénore. She complained to me of this change. 'What do you expect?' I said impatiently to her. 'I suppose you imagine you have done a lot for me; I must tell you, you are mistaken. I fail to understand your new mode of life. You used to live in retirement; you fled from wearisome society; you avoided those endless conversations which continue precisely because they should never have begun. It would seem that, in asking you to receive me, I have obtained the same favour for all the world. I must confess that, having seen you formerly so prudent, I did not expect to find you so frivolous.'

I discerned in Ellénore's features a feeling of displeasure and sadness. 'My dear Ellénore,' I said, becoming immediately more gentle, 'do I not deserve to be distinguished from the thousand and one tiresome people who throng around you? Has friendship no secrets? Is it not timid and easily slighted in the midst of a noisy crowd?'

Ellénore feared to show herself inflexible, lest the imprudence which alarmed her on her account and on mine should be renewed. She no longer entertained in her heart the idea of breaking off our friendship: she consented to see me sometimes alone.

The strict rules she had prescribed for me were then rapidly modified. She allowed me to describe my love; she gradually became familiar with this language: soon she confessed she loved me.

I passed many hours at her feet, proclaiming I was the happiest of men, lavishing on her countless assurances of tenderness, devotion and eternal respect.

She told me of how she had suffered in trying to stay
away from me; how many times she had hoped I would
discover her despite her efforts; how the slightest noise
striking her ears seemed to announce my arrival; what
emotions, what joys, what misgivings she felt on seeing me again. It was because of her mistrust of herself,
and in order to reconcile the fondness of her heart
with prudence, that she had given herself up to social
distractions and had sought the company she used to
flee. I made her repeat the least details, and this account of a few weeks seemed to us to be that of a whole
lifetime. Love makes up for the lack of long memories
by a sort of magic. All other affections need a past;
love creates a past which envelops us, as if by en-
chantment. It gives us, so to speak, a consciousness of
having lived for years with a being who, not so long
ago, was almost a stranger. Love is only a luminous
point, and nevertheless it seems to take complete possession of time. A few days ago it did not exist, soon
it will exist no more; but as long as it exists, it sheds
light on the period which went before, just as it will
on that which will follow.

This calm state, however, did not last. Ellénore was
the more on her guard against her weakness in that
she was pursued by the memory of her transgressions:
and my imagination, my desires, a theory, of the fatuity
of which I was not even aware, revolted against the
idea of this kind of love. Always timid, often angry,
I complained, and flew into a rage and heaped reproaches on Ellénore. More than once she made up
her mind to break off a tie which only brought disquiet and disturbance to her life, and as many times,
I calmed her with my prayers, my disavowals and tears.

'Ellénore,' I wrote to her one day, 'you cannot know
all that I suffer. Near to you or far from you, I am
equally unhappy. During the hours which separate us,
I wander aimlessly, bowed under the burden of an
existence which I do not know how to bear. Society
wearies me, solitude overwhelms me. Those who are
nothing to me, who observe me, who know nothing
of what preoccupies me, who look at me with curiosity
but no interest, with astonishment but no pity, those

men who dare to speak to me of something else than you, inflict a mortal pain on me. I shun them; but once I am alone, I gasp in vain for air to relieve the oppression in my breast. I throw myself on the ground which ought to open and swallow me up for ever; I lay my head on the cold stone which ought to calm the burning fever which consumes me. I drag myself to that hill from which your house can be seen; I stay there, with my eyes fixed on the retreat which I shall never share with you. And to think that if I had met you sooner, you could have been mine! I should have pressed in my arms the only creature which nature has formed after my own heart, after my heart which has suffered so much because it was seeking you and only found you too late!

'When these hours of delirium have finally passed, and the moment arrives when I can see you, trembling, I take the road to your house. I fear lest all those I meet should guess the feelings which I bear in me. I stop. I walk slowly. I retard the moment of happiness which is threatened by everything and which I always fear I am on the point of losing. It is an imperfect and troubled happiness against which each moment, every fateful incident, jealous look and tyrannical caprice, and, indeed your own will, may be conspiring. When I reach your door, when I begin to open it, a new terror seizes me: I advance like a guilty person, begging mercy of every object which meets my sight, as if they were all enemies, as if everything envied me the hour of felicity which I am again to enjoy. The slightest noise frightens me, the least movement about me terrifies me, the sound of my own footsteps makes me retreat. When almost in your presence, I am still afraid that some obstacle may suddenly arise between you and me.

'At last I see you, I see you and can breathe; I gaze at you and I stop like a fugitive who has reached a sanctuary which will save him from death. But at the very moment, when my whole being is impelled towards you, when I have such need to rest and recover from all these anxieties, to lay my head on your knees, to let my tears flow freely, even at that moment, I am

obliged to restrain myself violently and, at your very
side, to live a life of effort. Not a moment in which I
can unburden myself, not a moment of abandon! Your
eyes observe me. You are embarrassed, almost offended,
at my state. A mysterious constraint has followed on
those delightful hours in which you at least confessed
your love to me. Time flies, new interests solicit you;
you never forget them; you never put off the moment
of my going. Strangers come: I am no longer allowed
to look at you; I feel I must leave to escape from the
suspicions which surround me. I leave you, more
agitated, more torn, more crazed than before; I leave
you and I fall back into that fearful isolation in which
I struggle without a soul on whom I can lean and
rest a single moment.'

Ellénore had never been loved in this fashion. Count
P—— had a true affection for her, much gratitude for
her devotion, much respect for her character; but there
was always in his manner a shade of superiority over a
woman who had given herself publicly to him without
his having to marry her. He could have contracted more
honourable matches, according to public opinion: he
never said so to her, perhaps he never said so to himself;
but what is not said exists none the less, and everything
that is can be divined. Ellénore, till now, had had no
notion of that passionate feeling, of that existence lost
in hers of which my very rages, my injustices and reproaches were indisputable proofs. Her resistance had
inflamed all my senses, all my ideas: I again gave way to
the passionate outbursts which frightened her to a sub-
missiveness, a tenderness and an idolatrous veneration.
I considered her as a celestial creature. My love was akin
to worship and had the more charm for her since she
never ceased to fear being humiliated in the opposite
way. At last she gave herself to me without reservation.

Woe betide the man who in the first moments of a
love affair does not believe that liaison to be eternal!
Woe betide him who preserves a fatal foreknowledge,
even in the arms of the mistress he has just acquired,
and foresees he will be able to leave her! A woman
whose heart has carried her away has, in that moment,
something moving and sacred. It is not pleasure, it is

not nature, it is not our senses which corrupt; it is the calculations to which society accustoms us, and the reflections to which experience gives rise. I loved, I respected Ellénore a thousand times more when she had given herself to me. I walked with pride amongst men; I looked round at them with a proud look. The very air I breathed gave me pleasure. I rushed to meet nature half-way, to thank her for the unhoped for, the immense blessing she had deigned to grant me.

IV WHO CAN DESCRIBE THE CHARM OF LOVE? THAT conviction that we have found the being who was destined by nature to be ours, that hidden illumination of life, that new value attaching to the slightest circumstances, those swift hours, the details of which elude us in retrospect through their very sweetness, leaving in our mind only a long trail of happiness; that playful gaiety which occasionally mingles for no reason with our general feeling of tenderness; in our love's presence such pleasure, in her absence such hope; such aloofness to all vulgar cares, such feeling of superiority towards all our surroundings and of certainty that, on the plane on which we are living, society can no longer touch us; and that mutual understanding which divines each thought and responds to each emotion—the charm of love! Those who have known the charm of love cannot describe it!

For pressing business reasons, Count P—— had to go away for six weeks. I spent that time with Ellénore almost without a break. Her attachment to me seemed to have increased on account of the sacrifice she had made for me. She never let me leave her without trying to detain me. When I was about to depart, she would ask me when I would return. Two hours of separation were unbearable to her. She anxiously fixed the exact moment of my return. I consented joyously to this, I was grateful to her. Her feeling for me made me happy.

The ordinary interests of life will not, however, yield arbitrarily to all our desires. It was not always convenient for me to have all my movements mapped out with every moment reckoned in advance. I was forced to dispatch all my affairs with the greatest haste and to sever most of my ties of friendship. I did not know what to reply to my acquaintances when they suggested our meeting, though, if my situation had been a normal one, I should have had no reason to refuse. It was not that, when I was with Ellénore, I regretted these social pleasures in which I had never been particularly interested, but I would rather she had let me give them up of my own free-will. I should have had far more pleasure in returning to her of my own accord if I did not constantly have to remind myself that the time had come, that she was waiting for me, and if the idea of her unhappiness did not mingle with the happiness I anticipated on seeing her again.

Ellénore was undoubtedly a source of keen pleasure in my life, but she no longer represented a goal: she had become a bond. Moreover, I was afraid of compromising her. My continual presence must have astonished her children and those of her friends who could observe me. I shuddered to think I might upset her life. I felt we could not be united for ever and that it was a sacred duty for me to respect her peace of mind; I therefore counselled prudence and at the same time assured her of my love. But the more I gave her advice of this kind, the less she was inclined to heed what I said.

I was also terribly afraid of grieving her. As soon as I saw an expression of pain on her face, her will became mine. I was never at ease save when she was pleased with me. When, by dint of insisting on the necessity of absenting myself for a brief moment, I managed to leave her, I was pursued everywhere by the idea of the pain I had caused her. A fever of remorse took possession of me, increasing with every minute till it became irresistible; I flew back to her, looking forward to consoling and appeasing her. But as I approached her house, a feeling of ill-temper at this strange domination mingled with my other sentiments.

Ellénore herself was violent. I believe she felt for me
what she had felt for no one else. In her previous re-
lationships, her feelings had been wounded because of
her painful consciousness of dependence; with me, she
was perfectly at ease because on a footing of perfect
equality, she had regained her self-respect through a
love devoid of calculation and self-interest; she knew I
was sure she loved me for myself alone. But because
of her complete abandon with me, she would not disguise any of her feelings; and when I entered her
room, out of patience at having to return sooner than
I wanted to, I found her sad and irritated. Away from
her, I had suffered for two hours at the idea that she
was grieving through being away from me; and I
suffered two hours more at her side before I was able
to pacify her.

However, I was not unhappy; I used to tell myself
it was sweet to be loved, even in so exacting a way;
I felt it was doing her some good; to me her happiness
was essential and I knew I was essential to her happiness.

Besides, though the vague idea that, by the very
nature of things, this liaison could not last was in
many respects a sad one, it nevertheless served to calm
me in my fits of weariness or impatience. Several considerations, such as Ellénore's ties with Count P——, the
differences in our ages and situations, the fact that the
time of my departure, already postponed for various
reasons, was now imminent—all these things compelled
me to give and to receive as much happiness as was still
possible. I felt certain of the years to come and did not
argue about the days.

Count P—— returned. He was not slow to become
suspicious of my relations with Ellénore; each day, he
received me with a colder and darker expression. I
spoke forcefully to Ellénore of the dangers she was
running; I begged her to let me interrupt my visits for
several days; I emphasized the importance of her reputation, her fortune and her children. She listened to
me a long while in silence; she was as pale as death.
'In any case,' she said at last, 'you will soon be leaving; let us not anticipate that moment; do not worry

about me. Let us rather gain time, if only days and hours: days and hours, that is all I ask. Some vague presentiment, Adolphe, tells me I shall die in your arms.'

We therefore continued to live as before, with myself always anxious, Ellénore always sad and Count P——taciturn and preoccupied. At last, the letter I was waiting for arrived. I took it to Ellénore. 'Already!' she said, after reading it. 'I did not think it would be so soon.' Then, bursting into tears, she took my hand and said: 'Adolphe, you see I cannot live without you; I do not know what will become of me in the future, but I beg you not to leave yet. Find some excuse for staying. Ask your father to let you prolong your stay another six months. Six months, that is all. Is that so long to ask?' I wanted to make her change her mind; but she wept so bitterly, she was trembling so violently, her features bore the stamp of a suffering so heart-rending, that I could not continue. I threw myself at her feet, I pressed her in my arms, I protested my love for her, and I went to write to my father. And I did, in fact, write while still moved by Ellénore's suffering. I advanced a thousand reasons for delaying my departure; I pointed out how useful it would be to continue to attend several courses in D—— which I had been unable to follow in Göttingen; and when I sent my letter to the post, I did so ardently desiring my father's consent to what I was asking.

I returned that evening to Ellénore. She was waiting on a sofa. Count P—— was near the fire-place, somewhat apart from her; the two children were at the back of the room. They were not playing, but their faces showed the astonishment of children when they become aware of some agitation in others without suspecting the cause. I let Ellénore know by a gesture that I had done what she wanted me to. Her eyes lit up with a joy which was soon effaced. We said nothing. The silence was becoming embarrassing for all three of us. At last, the Count said to me: 'I am told you are ready to go.' I said I was not aware of this and he replied: 'It seems to me that, at your age, one ought to lose no time in taking up a career.' 'However,' he added, looking at Ellénore, 'perhaps everybody here does not think the same as I do.'

My father's reply was not long in coming. I opened his letter, trembling at the thought of the pain a refusal would cause Ellénore. I even thought I should share that pain with equal bitterness. But on reading the consent my father granted me, all the drawbacks in prolonging my stay suddenly occurred to me. 'Another six months of torture and constraint!' I cried. 'Six months in which I shall offend the man who befriended me and expose the woman who loves me to insult; I may well cause her to lose the only situation in which she can live peacefully and live esteemed; I am deceiving my father. And why? In order to avoid braving a moment of pain which is inevitable, sooner or later! Do we not experience every particle of this pain each day? I am only doing Ellénore harm; my sentiment for her, as it is at present, cannot satisfy her. I am sacrificing myself for her without contributing anything to her happiness. And I, myself, am leading a useless life, without any independence, without a free moment; I cannot breathe one hour in peace.'

I entered Ellénore's room, absorbed in these reflections. I found her alone. 'I am staying a further six months,' I said. 'That is rather a dry way of announcing the news.' 'Because, I must confess, I greatly fear the consequences of this delay to you and to me.' 'It seems to me they cannot be very unfortunate as far as you are concerned.' 'Ellénore, you know very well, my chief concern has never been myself.' 'Nor the happiness of others.'

The conversation had taken a stormy turn. Ellénore's feelings were hurt at my having regrets at a time when she believed I should share her joy. My feelings were hurt at her triumph over my previous resolution. The scene was violent. We burst into mutual reproaches. Ellénore accused me of having deceived her, of having had only a passing liking for her, of alienating the Count's affection for her and, in the eyes of the world, of throwing her back into the dubious situation from which she had tried all her life to escape. I was angered to see how she turned against me all that I had done

out of obedience to her will and out of fear of causing
her pain. I complained of the severe constraints imposed on me, of my youth wasted in inaction, of her
despotic ruling over my every movement. Whilst speaking thus, I saw her face suddenly bathed in tears. I
stopped, I retraced my steps, I retracted and explained.
We embraced: but a first blow had been struck, a first
barrier cleared. We had both made irreparable statements; we could pass them over in silence but not
forget them. There are things one does not say for a
long time, but, once they are said, one never stops repeating them.

We lived thus for four months in a forced intimacy
which was sometimes sweet, but never completely free.
We found pleasure in it but no more charm. Ellénore,
however, showed no sign of turning against me. After
our sharpest quarrels, she was just as anxious to see
me again, she fixed the time for our meeting with as
great a care as if our union were the most peaceful and
tender imaginable. I often thought my very conduct
helped to maintain Ellénore in this mood. If I had
loved her as she loved me, she would have been less
anxious on my behalf and would herself have reflected
on the dangers she was running. But any prudence
was repugnant to her because prudence came from me.
She did not count her sacrifices because she was busy
making me accept them; she did not have time to let
her ardour for me cool because all her time and energy
were employed in keeping her hold on me. The new
date fixed for my departure was approaching and, when
I thought of this, I felt a mixture of pleasure and regret
similar to that felt by a man who is certain of recovering his health at the price of a painful operation.

One morning, Ellénore wrote asking me to go to
her at once. 'The Count,' she said, 'forbids my seeing
you. I will not obey this tyrannical order. I followed
this man into exile, I saved his fortune for him; I have
served his every interest. He can do without me now.
But I cannot do without you.' One can easily guess
what earnest entreaties I made to dissuade her from
a plan which was inconceivable to me. I spoke of public
opinion. 'Public opinion has never been just towards

me,' she replied. 'I have fulfilled my duties for ten
years better than any woman and yet public opinion
has none the less denied me the position I deserved.'
I reminded her of her children. 'My children belong
to Count P——. He has acknowledged them. They will
be only too happy to forget a mother whose shame is
all they can share.' My entreaties became more earnest.
'Listen,' she said. 'If I break with the Count, will you
refuse to see me? Will you?' she insisted, taking my
arm with a violence which made me shudder. 'No, of
course not,' I replied. 'And the greater your misfortune,
the more devoted I shall be. But think——' 'I have
thought of everything,' she interrupted. 'He will soon
be returning. Go away now and do not come back
here.'

I spent the rest of the day in a state of unutterable
anguish. Two days passed without my hearing anything
of Ellénore. I suffered at not knowing what her fate
could be; I suffered even at not seeing her, and I was
astonished at the pain which this privation caused in
me. I hoped, however, that she would abandon a resolve which gave me such fears for her, and I began
to delude myself that she might have done this when
a woman handed me a note from Ellénore, begging
me to go and see her in a certain street and house on
the third floor.

I ran to this place, still hoping that, being unable to
receive me at the Count's, she wanted to have a last
talk with me somewhere else. I found her arranging
things as if settling there for good. She came to me
with a glad but timid air, trying to read my reaction
in my eyes. 'I have broken away completely,' she said.
'I am perfectly free. My own fortune brings in an income of seventy-five louis. That is enough for me. You
will be staying another six weeks. When you leave, I
shall perhaps be able to follow you. You will perhaps
come and see me.' And, as if she feared to hear my
reply, she immediately went into a host of details
concerning her plans.

In a thousand ways, she tried to persuade me that
she would be happy, that she had sacrificed nothing
and that the course she had chosen suited her, even

without considering me. She was obviously making a great effort and only half believed what she was saying. She was intoxicating herself with her own words for fear of hearing mine; she was endeavouring to prolong what she had to say in order to put off the moment when my objections would plunge her back into despair. I could not find it in my heart to make a single objection. I accepted the sacrifice, I thanked her for it; I told her it made me happy. I said far more: I assured her I had always hoped for an irreparable decision, which would make it my duty never to leave her. I attributed my hesitation to a delicacy which prevented me from consenting to anything which would upset her situation. Briefly, my only concern was to remove from her mind all pain, all fear, all regret, all doubts about my feelings towards her. While I was speaking to her, I considered nothing beyond this aim and I was sincere in my promises.

V ELLÉNORE'S SEPARATION FROM THE COUNT produced an effect which could readily be imagined. In a single moment she lost the fruit of ten years' devotion and constancy: she was taken to be like all the women of her class who yield without qualms to every passing fancy. Her abandonment of her children caused her to be looked upon as an unnatural mother, and women of irreproachable reputation remarked, with much satisfaction, that the neglect of the most essential virtue of their sex was soon followed by the neglect of all the others. At the same time, they pitied her in order to have the pleasure of blaming me. My conduct was considered that of a seducer, of an ungrateful person who had violated the hospitality he had received and who had, to satisfy the whim of a moment, sacrificed the peaceful life of two people, one of whom he should have treated with respect and the other with consideration.

Some of my father's friends made serious representations to me; others, being less free with me, made me feel their disapproval by indirect insinuations. On the other hand, the younger men, delighted at the skill with which I had supplanted the Count, congratulated me in numerous jokes which I was unable to suppress. They promised to follow my example. I cannot describe what I had to endure both in the way of harsh strictures and shameful praises. I am persuaded that if I had loved Ellénore, I should have managed to bring opinion round in her favour and in mine. The power of true feeling is such that it can silence false interpretations and artificial conventions. But I was only a weak, grateful and dominated man; I was sustained by no impulse from the heart. I therefore expressed myself with embarrassment; I tried to bring the conversation to an end and, if it still continued, I would end it with a few harsh words which made it clear I was ready to start a quarrel. In fact, I would much rather have fought than replied.

Ellénore soon noticed that opinion was roused against her. Two of the Count's women relations, whom he had forced by his powerful influence to show friendship for her, broke with her with the greatest ostentation; they were only too happy to give way behind the veil of austere moral principles to the spite which they had had to restrain for so long. The men continued to see Ellénore; but a certain note of familiarity crept in, showing she was now without a powerful protector and no longer justified by an almost consecrated union. Some visited her, because, as they said, they had always known her; others because she was still beautiful and her recent light conduct had revived aspirations which they did not try to disguise from her. They all gave reasons for their relationship with her; in other words, they all thought that this relationship needed an excuse.

The unhappy Ellénore thus found herself in the position above which she had tried all her life to rise. Everything conspired to vex her spirit and wound her pride. In those who deserted her, she saw a proof of contempt; in the assiduity of the others, a sign of some insulting hope. She suffered in solitude and was ashamed in society. Ah! I suppose I should have consoled her; I ought to have held her close to me and said: 'Let us live for one another and forget people who misunderstand us; let us be happy in our own mutual esteem and love—that is all we need.' I tried this method, but what power to revive a dying sentiment has a resolve inspired by a mere sense of duty?

Ellénore and I concealed our real feelings from one another. She did not dare confide in me the troubles arising from a sacrifice for which she knew very well I had not asked. I had accepted that sacrifice: I did not dare to complain of a misfortune I had foreseen but which I had not had the strength to forestall. We both, therefore, remained silent about the one thought which we constantly had in mind. We were lavish in our caresses, we spoke of love; but we spoke of love for fear of speaking of other things.

As soon as a secret exists between two hearts that love each other, as soon as one of them is determined to hide a single idea from the other, the charm is broken, the happiness destroyed. Anger, injustice, even forgetfulness can be repaired, but dissimulation generates in love a foreign matter which changes its nature and appears to poison it.

With strange inconsequence, whilst indignantly rejecting the slightest insinuation against Ellénore, I myself also wronged her in my general conversation. I had submitted to her will, but domination by women had become abhorrent to me. I ceaselessly decried their weakness, their exacting nature, the despotism of their suffering. I made show of the harshest principles; and the same man who could not withstand a tear, who yielded at the mere sight of sadness and who, when alone, was haunted by the picture of the suffering he had caused, yet showed himself in all his talk to be contemptuous and pitiless. All my direct praises of Ellénore could not destroy the impression produced by such talk. I was hated, she was pitied but not esteemed. She was blamed for not inspiring in her lover

more consideration for her sex and more respect for
the ties of the heart.

A man who had constantly visited Ellénore and
who, since her separation from Count P——, had shown
her the liveliest passion, had forced her, through his
indiscreet persecutions, to refuse to admit him. He
thereupon permitted himself outrageous sarcasms concerning her which I felt I could not let pass. We
fought. I wounded him dangerously and I was also
wounded.

I cannot describe the mixture of emotion, terror,
gratitude and love which were depicted in Ellénore's
face when she saw me after this incident. She moved
into my rooms, despite all my injunctions; she did not
leave me a single instant until I became convalescent.
She read to me during the day and watched over me
for the best part of the night; she observed my slightest
movement, she anticipated all my wishes; the ingenuity
of her kindness sharpened her faculties and doubled
her strength. She assured me unceasingly that she
would not have outlived me; I was filled with affection
and torn by remorse. I wished I could have found in
me some way to reward her for so constant and tender
an attachment; I called to my aid memories, imagination, even reason and my sense of duty—in vain! The
difficulties of the situation, the certainty that in the
future we should be separated, and perhaps some obscure revolt against a bond I was unable to break,
preyed upon my mind. I reproached myself with the
ingratitude which I endeavoured to hide from her.
I was distressed when she seemed to question the love
which was so necessary to her; I was no less distressed
when she seemed to believe in it. I felt she was better
than I; I despised myself for not being worthy of her.
It is a fearful misfortune not to be loved when you
love; but it is a much greater misfortune to be loved
passionately when you love no longer. The life I had
just exposed on Ellénore's behalf I would have given
many times over to make her happy without me.

The six months my father had granted had elapsed.
I had to think of leaving. Ellénore did not oppose my
departure, she did not even try to delay it; but she

made me promise that I would return to her two
months later or allow her to come to me; I solemnly
made this promise. I would have made any promise in
a moment like this when I could see she was struggling
with her feelings and concealing her pain. She could
have asked me not to leave her; I knew at the bottom
of my heart her tears would not have gone unanswered.
I was grateful to her for not exerting her power; I
seemed to love her the more for this. Moreover, I
myself could not leave without keen regret a being
who showed me such single-minded devotion. There
is something so profound in prolonged affairs. They
become unconsciously so intimate a part of our existence! A long while ahead, we calmly plan to break
them off; we fancy we are waiting impatiently for the
time to put this plan into effect: but when the moment arrives, it fills us with terror: and such is the
strangeness of our miserable heart that it is with horrible anguish we leave those by whose side we lived
without pleasure.

During my absence, I wrote regularly to Ellénore.
I was torn between the fear that my letters might
cause her pain and the desire only to depict my true
sentiments. I would have liked her to understand
through intuition, but to do so without being unduly
distressed; and I congratulated myself when I managed
to substitute the language of affection, friendship and
devotion for that of love. But suddenly I pictured
Ellénore alone and sad, and my letters her only consolation; and, at the end of two cold and formal pages,
I would swiftly add a few passionate or tender lines of
a sort likely to deceive her once more. In this way,
without ever saying enough to satisfy her, I always said
enough to delude her. What a strange piece of false-
ness! Its very success turned against me. It prolonged
my anguish and was unbearable to me!

I anxiously counted the days and hours as they
passed; I wished to slow down the march of time; I
trembled as I perceived the day approaching when I
should have to fulfil my promise. I could think of no
way of leaving, and I could discover no way in which
Ellénore could settle in the same town as myself. Per-

haps, to be quite honest, I did not desire to. I compared
my independent and peaceful life with the rash, uneasy and tormented existence to which I was condemned
by her passion. I found it so enjoyable to be free,
going and coming, leaving the house and returning
without anyone taking the slightest notice. Tired by
her love, I was, so to speak, basking in the indifference
of others.

I dared not, however, let Ellénore suspect that I
would like to abandon our plan. She had understood
from my letters that it would be difficult for me to
leave my father; she, therefore, wrote to me that she
had begun to prepare for her departure. For a long
time I did not oppose her decision; I made no definite
reply on this subject. I told her vaguely that I should
always be delighted to know, then I added, to *make*
her happy: such sorry equivocation and so involved
a language! I groaned to see it so obscure and feared
to make it clearer!

At last I decided to speak frankly to her; I felt I
owed it to her; I roused my conscience against my
weakness; I fortified myself against the idea of her pain
with the idea of her peace. I paced up and down my
room, reciting aloud what I proposed to tell her. But,
scarcely had I written a few lines than my mood
changed: I no longer saw in my words the meaning
they were meant to convey, but the effect they could
not fail to produce; and, as if, despite myself, a super-
natural power guided and controlled my hand, I confined myself to advising putting off the visit for several
months. I had not said what I was thinking. My letter
bore no stamp of sincerity. The arguments I put forward were weak, because they were not the true ones.

Ellénore's reply was violent. She was indignant at
my desire not to see her. What did she ask of me? To
live near me unrecognized. What could I fear from
her presence in a secret haunt in the middle of a large
town where no one knew her? She had sacrificed everything on my account: her fortune, her children, her
reputation; the only reward she wanted for these sacrifices was to wait for me like a humble slave, to spend
a few minutes with me each day, to enjoy the few

moments I could give her. She had resigned herself to two months' absence, not that this absence seemed necessary, but because I appeared to wish for it; and when, by dint of painfully adding one day to another, she had reached the end of the period I myself had fixed, I suggested she should start this long torture all over again! She might have been mistaken in me, she might have given away her life to a hard and heartless man; I was the master of my actions; but I was not a master who had a right to force her to suffer, abandoned by the one for whom she had sacrificed all.

Ellénore herself soon followed her letter; she informed me of her arrival. I went to her with the firm resolve to show her much joy; I was anxious to reassure her heart and to give her, momentarily at least, happiness or calm of mind. But her feelings had been hurt; she observed me mistrustfully: she soon noticed what an effort I was making; she exasperated my pride by her reproaches; she violently attacked my character and showed me and my weakness in such a miserable light that I was repelled more by her than by myself. An insensate rage took possession of us: all consideration was thrown aside, all delicacy forgotten. It was as if we had been set one against the other by furies. We applied to each other all that the most implacable hatred in the world had invented against us; and these two unhappy beings who alone knew each other, could understand and console, and render justice to each other, appeared to be two irreconcilable enemies bent on tearing one another to pieces.

We parted after a scene lasting three hours; and, for the first time in our life, we parted without an explanation and without making amends. Scarcely had I left Ellénore than a deep anguish replaced my anger. I found myself in a kind of stupor, utterly dazed by what had happened. The words I had used I repeated with amazement; I could not understand my conduct; I wondered what frenzy could have possessed me.

It was very late; I dared not go back to Ellénore. I counted on seeing her early the next morning and went home. In my father's house, there was a large gathering and it was easy for me to stay apart and hide my agitation. When we were alone, my father said to me: 'I am told Count P——'s former mistress is in this town. I have always allowed you great liberty and never wanted to know anything about your affairs; but it is undesirable at your age publicly to proclaim a mistress; I warn you I have taken steps to make her leave the town.' Having said these words, he walked away. I followed him to his bedroom; he signed to me to leave him. 'Father,' I said, 'as God is my witness, I want her to be happy. If that desire can be fulfilled, I will consent never to see her again; but take care what you do. Thinking you are separating me from her, you may well attach me to her for ever.'

I immediately summoned to my room a manservant who had accompanied me in my travels and who knew of my liaison with Ellénore. I instructed him to find out at once what steps my father intended taking. He came back two hours later. My father's secretary had confided to him under the seal of secrecy that on the morrow Ellénore would receive an order to leave. 'Ellénore driven out!' I cried. 'Driven out in disgrace! She who came here only to see me, she whose heart I have broken, she whose tears I saw flowing whilst I showed no pity! Where will she rest her head, that poor unhappy woman, wandering alone in the world amongst people whose esteem I have torn from her? To whom will she tell her suffering?'

My mind was soon made up. I found my servant; I showered gold and promises on him. I ordered a post-chaise for six o'clock the following morning at the town gates. My head was full of plans for my eternal reunion with Ellénore; I loved her more than ever before; all my affection for her returned; I was proud to be her protector. I was longing to hold her in my arms; love had completely invaded my mind; there was a fever in my brain, my heart, and my senses which transformed my whole existence. If at that moment Ellénore had wished to leave me, I should have died at her feet to prevent her from doing so.

Day came; I ran to Ellénore. She was still in bed, having spent the night weeping; her eyes were still wet, her hair disheveled; she was surprised to see me enter. 'Look,' I said, 'we must go.' She wanted to reply. 'We must go,' I insisted. 'Is there anyone else in the world to protect and befriend you? Are my arms not your only sanctuary?' She demurred. 'I have important reasons, private reasons,' I added. 'In heaven's name, follow me.' I bore her away.

During the journey, I smothered her with caresses, I pressed her to my heart, I replied to her questions only by kissing her. But eventually, I told her that having discovered my father's intentions of separating us, I had felt I could not be happy without her; that I wanted to devote the rest of my life to her and be united to her by every kind of tie. At first, her gratitude was intense; but she soon detected contradictions in my story. By dint of entreaties, she drew the truth from me; her joy vanished, a dark cloud came over her face.

'Adolphe,' she said, 'you are deceiving yourself; you are generous, you are devoted to me because I am being persecuted; you believe you are moved by love but you are only moved by pity.' Why did she pronounce those fatal words? Why did she reveal a secret I preferred not to know? I endeavoured to reassure her and perhaps I managed to do so; but the truth had transfixed my heart; the first impulse was broken; I was determined to continue with my sacrifice but I was no happier for that, and I already had a new preoccupation which I was reduced to concealing.

VI WHEN WE HAD ARRIVED AT THE FRONTIER, I wrote to my father. My letter was respectful but it had an underlying bitterness. I bore him ill will for having tightened my bonds whilst claiming to loosen them. I informed him that I would never leave Ellénore until such time as she was suitably settled and no longer in need of me. I begged him not to persecute her and so force me to remain

always attached to her. I waited for his reply before
deciding on the style of living we should adopt.

'You are twenty-four,' his answer ran. 'I shall not
bring my authority to bear against you—an authority
which is near its end and which I have never used; I
shall even conceal to the best of my ability the strange
step you have taken; I shall spread the rumour that
you have left on my instructions and on my behalf. I
shall make you a liberal allowance for your expenses.
You, yourself, will soon feel that the life you are leading is not the one which suits you. Your place in the
world, by your birth, talents and fortune, should be
a very different one from that of companion to a
homeless woman without a country. Your letter proves
to me already that you are not pleased with yourself.
Reflect, then, that nothing is gained by prolonging a
situation of which you are ashamed. You are uselessly
wasting the best years of your youth and that loss is
irreparable.'

My father's letter pierced me with a thousand dagger
thrusts. I had told myself the same things countless
times; I had been countless times ashamed of spending
my life in obscurity and inaction. I would have preferred reproaches and threats; I should then have felt
some glory in resisting them and in the necessity of
gathering all my strength to defend Ellénore from the
dangers which would have beset her. But there were
no dangers; I was perfectly free; and that freedom
served only to make me bear even less patiently the
yoke I appeared to have chosen myself.

We settled in Caden, a little town in Bohemia. I
repeated to myself that, since I had assumed responsibility for Ellénore's fate, I must not make her suffer.
I managed to restrain myself; I hid in my bosom the
slightest signs of dissatisfaction and used all the resources of my mind to create an artificial gaiety to
veil my deep sadness. This effort had a surprising effect
on me. We are such volatile creatures that we finally
feel the sentiments we feign. I partly forgot the sorrows
I was concealing. My perpetual joking dissipated my
own melancholy; and the assurances of love on which

I fed Ellénore instilled in my heart a sweet emotion which closely resembled love.

From time to time importunate memories besieged my mind. When alone, I gave myself up to fits of uneasiness; I made thousands of strange plans to flee from the cirle in which I was out of place. But I put these impressions from my mind as so many bad dreams. Ellénore appeared happy; how could I possibly upset her happiness? Nearly five months passed in this way.

One day, I saw that Ellénore was agitated and trying to conceal her anxiety from me. After much pleading, she made me promise that I would not contest the decision she had made and then she confessed that the Count had written to her: he had won his lawsuit; with gratitude he recalled the services she had rendered him and their intimacy of ten years' standing. He was offering her half his fortune, not to be reunited—that was no longer possible—but on condition she left the ungrateful and perfidious man who had separated them. 'I have answered him,' she said, 'and you may be sure I refused.'

I was only too sure of this. I was touched, but in despair at this new sacrifice which Ellénore was making on my behalf. Be that as it may, I did not dare to make any objection: my attempts in this direction had always been so fruitless! I went away to reflect on the course I should choose. It was clear to me that our ties would have to be broken. They were painful to me and harmful to her; I was the one obstacle which prevented her from recovering a fitting position in the world and the consideration which follows sooner or later on opulence; I was the one barrier between her and her children; I no longer had any excuse in my own eyes. To yield to her in these circumstances was no longer generosity but a sinful weakness. I had promised my father I would become independent again as soon as I ceased to be necessary to Ellénore. And, moreover, it was time that I embarked on a career, began a life of action, acquired some claim to the esteem of my fellow men and put my faculties to some worthy use.

I went back to Ellénore, believing myself to be un-shakable in my design of forcing her not to reject the Count's offer, and to declare, if need be, that I no longer loved her. 'My dear,' I said to her, 'we struggle for a time against our destiny, but we always end by giving way. The laws of society are stronger than the will of men; the most powerful sentiments can be shattered on the fatality of circumstances. It is vain to persist in consulting only one's heart; sooner or later, one is bound to listen to reason. I cannot keep you any longer in a position which is unworthy of you and of me; I cannot do so, either for your sake or for mine.' I was speaking without looking at Ellé-nore, I felt my ideas were becoming vague and my resolution weakening. I wanted to regain control of myself and continued in a hurried tone: 'I shall al-ways be your friend; I shall always have the profound-est affection for you. The two years we have been together will never fade from my memory; they will always be the happiest years of my life. But, Ellénore, I no longer feel that ecstasy of the senses, that invol-untary intoxication, that forgetting of all worldly in-terests, of all duties—I no longer feel love.'

I waited for her reply a long time without raising my eyes towards her; when at last I looked at her, she was motionless; she was gazing at every object about her as if she did not recognize any of them. I took her hand: it was cold. She pushed me away. 'What do you want of me?' she asked. 'Am I not alone, alone in the world, alone without a single being who understands me? What more have you to say to me? Have you not said everything? Is not everything finished, irrevoca-bly? Go, leave me: is not that what you want?' She rose to depart, but she tottered. I tried to catch her, but she fell unconscious at my feet. I raised her up, I kissed her, I brought her round. 'Ellénore,' I cried. 'Come back to life, come back to me; I love you with the tenderest love; I misled you so that you could make your choice more freely.' How inexplicably cred-ulous is the heart! Those simple words, contradicted by so many previous words, brought Ellénore back to life and to confidence; she made me repeat them several times: she seemed to breathe eagerly. She believed me: she intoxicated herself with her love which she took for ours; she confirmed her reply to the Count, and I found myself more deeply committed than before.

Three months later there occurred another possibility of a change in Ellénore's circumstances. Through one of those vicissitudes which are common to republics torn by factions, her father was recalled to Poland and reinstated in his property. Although he scarcely knew his daughter who, at the age of three, had been taken to France by her mother, he wanted her to settle with him. Only vague rumours concerning Ellénore's adventures had reached him in Russia where he had lived during the whole of his exile. Ellénore was his only child: he was afraid of being lonely, he wanted to be cared for: all he had desired was to discover the whereabouts of his daughter and, as soon as he had found them out, he invited her warmly to come to him.

Ellénore could not feel any real attachment for a father whom she did not remember having seen. Nevertheless, she felt it was her duty to obey; in this way, she would secure a considerable fortune for her children, and herself regain the position in society which she had lost through her misfortune and conduct; but she declared emphatically that she would not go to Poland unless I accompanied her. 'I am no longer', she said, 'of an age when the mind is open to new impressions. My father is a stranger to me. If I stay here, others will eagerly surround him: he will be quite as happy. My children have Count P——'s fortune. I know perfectly well I shall be blamed by most people and be considered an ungrateful daughter and heartless mother: but I have suffered too much; I am no longer young enough to be much affected by public opinion. If you think there is something hard in my decision, you have only yourself to blame, Adolphe. If I had any illusions about you, I might perhaps agree to a temporary separation, the bitterness of which would be tempered by the prospect of a sweet and lasting reunion; but you would like nothing better than to know I was two hundred leagues from here, happy and at peace, surrounded by a family and wealth. You would write me very rational letters; I can see them now; they would rend my heart; I do not wish to expose myself to that. I cannot have the consolation of believing that, by the sacrifice of my whole life, I have managed to inspire in you the sentiments I deserve; be that as it may, you have accepted that sacrifice. I already suffer enough from the dryness of your manner and coolness of our relations; I endure these sufferings you inflict on me; I do not wish to face any I can avoid.'

Ellénore's voice had a certain bitter, violent tone which indicated a firm determination rather than a deep and touching emotion. She had developed the habit of becoming irritated in advance when she had to ask something of me, as if I had already refused it. She could command my actions, but knew that my private judgment belied them. She would have liked to penetrate the inner sanctuary of my mind to break down the secret opposition which enraged her against me. I spoke to her of my situation, of my father's wish, of my own desire; I pleaded and grew angry. Ellénore was unshakable. I wanted to arouse her generosity, just as though love were not the most selfish of all sentiments and in consequence, when wounded, the least generous. I made a strange effort to excite her pity over the unhappiness I experienced in staying with her; I managed only to exasperate her. I promised to go and see her in Poland; but she saw in the promises I made without warmth or abandon only my impatience to leave her.

The first year of our stay in Caden had come to an end without any change in our situation. When Ellénore found me gloomy or dejected, she was at first distressed, then wounded, and she drew from me by her reproaches the confession of weariness which I hould have liked to conceal. On my part, when Ellénore appeared happy, I was irritated at seeing her enjoy a situation which cost me my happiness, and I upset her brief enjoyment by insinuations which enlightened her as to my inner feelings. We then attacked each other in turn with indirect remarks, after which we retracted with general protestations and vague self-justifications, and lapsed once more into silence. For we both knew so well what the other was going to say that we kept silent in order not to hear it. Sometimes one of us would be ready to give way, but we would miss the favourable opportunity for reconciliation. Our mistrustful and wounded hearts could no longer come together.

I often wondered why I continued in so painful a state: I told myself it was because, if I left Ellénore, she would follow me and I should have provoked a fresh sacrifice on her part. And I said finally that I should satisfy her a last time and, when I had returned her to her family circle, she could demand nothing further of me. I was about to propose that I should follow her to Poland when she received news that her father had suddenly died. He had appointed her his sole heir, but his will was contradicted by later letters which distant relatives threatened to turn to account. Ellénore, despite the lack of commerce between her and her father, was painfully affected by his death: she reproached herself with having abandoned him. Soon she fell to blaming me for this fault of hers. 'You have made me fail to perform a sacred duty,' she said. 'Now all that remains is my fortune: I can sacrifice that to you even more readily. But I shall certainly not go alone into a country where I shall only meet enemies.' 'I never wished to make you fail in any duty,' I replied. 'But I could have wished, I must confess, that you would deign to reflect that I too found it painful not performing mine; I have not managed to obtain that justice from you. I surrender, Ellénore; *your* interest outweighs all other considerations. We will leave together whenever you please.'

We did, in fact, set out. The distractions of the journey, the novelty of things we saw, the self-control we tried to exercise, did, from time to time, revive what remained of our former harmony. Accustomed to each other as we were over a long period, the various vicissitudes we had experienced together, caused every word, almost every gesture, to arouse memories which translated us into the past and filled us with an involuntary emotion, like lightning flashing through the night but not dispersing the general darkness. We were living, so to speak, on memories of our hearts which were sufficiently strong to make the idea of separation painful to us, but too weak to permit us to find happiness in being

united. I yielded to these emotions in order to relax
from my habitual constraint. I should have liked to give
Ellénore proof of my feelings which would make her
happy; sometimes, I used afresh the language of love;
but these emotions and this language resembled those
pale and faded leaves which, amongst some remaining
funereal vegetation, grow languidly on the branches of
an uprooted tree.

VII AS SOON AS SHE ARRIVED, ELLÉNORE SE-
cured her reinstatement in the disputed
property on condition that she did not
dispose of it before her case had been
judged. She settled in one of the residences.

In his letters to me, my father never broached any
question directly: he merely filled them with insinuations
against my journey. 'You informed me,' he wrote, 'that
you would not leave. You gave your reasons for not leaving at great length; I was therefore thoroughly convinced that you would leave. I can only pity you for the
way in which, with your independent nature, you always
do the opposite of what you intend. But I am not judg-
ing a situation with which I am imperfectly acquainted.
Until now, you seemed to me to be Ellénore's protector,
and, in that light, your behaviour had something noble
about it which elevated your character whatever the
nature of the person to whom you were attached. Today,
your relationship is not the same; instead of you protecting her, she is protecting you; you are living in her
house, you are a stranger whom she has introduced into
her family. I am not pronouncing judgment on a position which you have chosen; but, as it may have disadvantages for you, I would like to reduce them as far
as is in my power. I am writing to Baron T——, who
is our minister in the country of your adoption, to rec-
ommend you to him; I do not know if you will care to
avail yourself of this introduction; at any rate, do not

see in it anything but a proof of my zeal and in no wise an attack on your independence which you have always known how to defend successfully against your father.'

I stifled the reflections which this manner of writing induced in me. The lands where I lived with Ellénore were not very far from Warsaw; I went there to call on Baron T——. He received me in friendly fashion, asked me the reasons for my stay in Poland and questioned me about my plans. I did not know what to answer. After a few minutes of embarrassing conversation, he said to me: 'I am going to speak frankly: I know the reasons which brought you to this country, your father told me of them; I will even say that I understand them: the man does not exist who has not, some time in his life, been torn between the desire to break off an impossible liaison and the fear of afflicting a woman he has loved. The inexperience of youth causes you greatly to exaggerate the difficulties of such a position; you believe in the truth of all those demonstrations of grief which in the weak and passionate sex are the arms that replace all those of strength and reason. Your heart suffers, but your pride is flattered; and the very man who, in all good faith, imagines he is immolating himself to the despair he has caused, only sacrifices himself in fact to the illusions created by his own vanity. There is not one of the many passionate women in the world who has not proclaimed that she will die if abandoned; there is not one who is still alive and who has not found consolation.'

I wanted to interrupt him. 'I am sorry, my young friend,' he went on, 'if I express myself with too little regard for your feelings: but the favourable reports I have about you, the talents you seem to possess and the career you should be pursuing—everything makes it clear that I must disguise no facts. I can read your mind, despite you, and better than you; you are no longer in love with the woman who dominates you and drags you after her; if you loved her still you would not have come to me. You knew your father had written to me; it was easy for you to imagine what I had to say to you: you were not angry at hearing from my mouth arguments

which you repeat to yourself constantly but in vain.
Ellénore's reputation is far from being intact.'

'Please end this futile conversation,' I replied. 'Unfortunate circumstances attended Ellénore's early years;
false appearances may cause her to be judged unfavour-
ably: but I have known her for three years and there is
on this earth no higher-minded a person, no nobler a
character, no purer and more generous a heart than
hers.'

'As you will,' he answered. 'But those are shades of
interpretation to which public opinion pays no heed.
The facts are plain and they are public. Do you imagine
that by preventing me from reminding you of them, you
can destroy them? Listen,' he continued. 'In this world
one must know what one wants. Are you going to marry
Ellénore?'

'No, I don't think so,' I cried. 'She has never wished
for it herself.'

'What do you intend to do then? She is ten years older
than you; you are twenty-six; you will look after her for
another ten years; she will then be old; you will have
reached the middle of your life without having started
anything, nor achieved anything to satisfy you. Boredom
will overtake you and ill-temper will take possession of
her; each day she will become less pleasing to you; each
day you will become more necessary to her; and, despite
an illustrious birth, a brilliant fortune and a distinguished mind, you will vegetate in a corner of Poland,
forgotten by your friends, lost to fame and tormented by
a woman who, whatever you do, will never be contented
with you. I will add only one thing and then we will
never return to this topic which embarrasses you. Every
road is open to you: letters, arms, administration; you
can aspire to the most illustrious matches; you can
succeed in anything you like: but you must remember
that, between you and all forms of success, there is one
insurmountable obstacle—and that obstacle is Ellénore.'

'I felt, sir, that I owed it to you to listen to you in
silence,' I replied. 'But I also owe it to myself to declare
that you have not shaken my determination in the slightest degree. I repeat, no one but myself is in a position
to judge Ellénore: no one appreciates sufficiently the

trueness of her sentiments and the depth of her emotions. As long as she needs me, I shall stay by her. No success would console me for having left her unhappy; and even if my career had to be confined to protecting her, giving her support in her cares and surrounding her with my affection as a shield against the injustice of people who misunderstand her, I should still believe my life had not been spent in vain.'

I left when I had spoken these words: but who can explain to me by what fickleness of character the sentiment which dictated them had vanished even before I had finished pronouncing them? Returning on foot, I wanted to put off the moment when I should see again that Ellénore whom I had just defended; I crossed the town in haste; I longed to be alone.

On reaching open country, I slowed my pace and countless thoughts assailed me. Those baleful words: 'Between you and all forms of success, there is one insurmountable obstacle—and that obstacle is Ellénore', echoed around me. My mind lingered sadly on the time which had gone and would not return; I recalled my youthful hopes, the confidence with which I formerly believed I could command the future, the praise my first attempts called forth, a dawning reputation I saw glow and vanish. I repeated to myself the names of several of my fellow students whom I had treated with proud disdain and who, merely by virtue of dogged work and a regular life, had left me far behind on the road to fortune, consideration and fame: my inaction oppressed me.

Just as a miser pictures to himself as he gazes at the wealth he has amassed all the objects this wealth might buy, so I recognized in Ellénore the denial of all the success to which I might have aspired. It was not merely one career which I regretted; as I had tried none, I regretted them all. Never having put my powers to the test, I imagined them unbounded and I cursed them; I would have preferred nature to have made me weak and mediocre, in order to spare me at least the remorse of having voluntarily to degrade myself. All praise or approbation of my mind or knowledge seemed to me an intolerable reproach—like admiration of the powerful

limbs of an athlete who is shackled at the bottom of a
cell. If I wished to take heart again, and tell myself that
my active youth was not yet over, Ellénore's image
would rise in front of me like a ghost and cast me back
into nothingness; I had fits of anger against her and yet,
strangely enough, this anger did not lessen by one jot
my terror at the idea of distressing her.

Wearied by these bitter feelings, my mind suddenly
sought refuge in contrary sentiments. A few chance
words pronounced by Baron T—— on the possibility of
a quiet and peaceful marriage helped me to create the
ideal of a companion. I reflected on the peacefulness,
the consideration, and even the independence which
such a condition would represent; for, the bonds I had
been dragging after me for so long made me a thousand
times more dependent than an unknown but regularized
union could have done. I imagined my father's joy; I
felt an impatient desire to resume in my country and in
the society of my equals the place which was due to me;
I saw myself countering with an austere and irreproachable conduct all the condemnations which had been
pronounced against me in cold and frivolous spite, and
also all the reproaches which Ellénore heaped upon me.
'She is always accusing me of being hard, ungrateful
and of having no pity,' I said. 'Ah, had heaven granted
me a woman whom social conventions permitted me to
acknowledge and whom my father would not have been
ashamed to admit as his daughter, then, making her
happy would have been a source of infinite happiness
to me. My feelings are not appreciated because they are
hurt and wounded. Before anger and threats, my heart
refuses to show any of these delicate considerations
which are so imperiously demanded. But how sweet it
would have been for me to be able to indulge in them
with a dear companion in a regular and respected
manner of living! What have I not sacrificed for Ellénore? For her sake I left my home and family; for her
sake I have grieved my old father who is still lamenting
over me, far away; for her sake I am living in this place
where my youth slips away in solitude, without glory,
without honour, and without delight. Do not so many
sacrifices made without obligation and without love

prove what I could do with love and obligations? If I
fear so much to cause grief to a woman who only rules
me through that grief, with what care should I avoid
causing any sorrow or pain to a woman to whom I could
devote myself without remorse or reservation! Then,
people would see how different I could be from what I
now am! How swiftly and completely a bitterness, held
to be criminal because its cause is not known, would
fall from me! How grateful I should be to heaven and
how kindly disposed towards men!'

I spoke thus and my eyes filled with tears; memories
came to my mind, as it were, in floods; my relations with
Ellénore had made all these memories hateful. Everything which recalled my childhood, the places in which
I had spent my early years, my first playmates, the old
relatives who had first shown interest in me, tortured
and hurt me; I was reduced to avoiding like guilty
thoughts the most attractive images and most natural
desires. The companion that my imagination had suddenly created was, on the other hand, allied in my mind
with all these images and approved all these desires;
she was associated with all my duties, all my pleasures,
all my tastes; she linked my present life with that period
of my youth in which hope opened before me so vast a
future, a period from which Ellénore separated me by
a gulf.

The slightest details, the smallest objects recurred to
my mind; I could see once more the ancient castle where
I had lived with my father, the woods surrounding it,
the river which bathed its outer walls, the mountains on
the horizon. All these things appeared so real to me, so
full of life that they caused me to tremble in a way I
could scarcely bear; and beside them my imagination
placed a young and innocent creature who rendered
them more beautiful and gave them life and hope.
Plunged in this dream, I wandered, still with no fixed
plan and without admitting that I must break with
Ellénore, having only a vague and confused notion of
reality. I was in the state of a man overwhelmed with
sorrow and whom sleep has consoled with a dream, but
who feels the dream is about to end. I suddenly found
myself before Ellénore's house which I had uncon-

sciously approached; I stopped; I took another turning, glad to put off the moment when I should hear her voice again.

The light was failing: the sky was cloudless; the countryside was becoming deserted; men had ceased their labours; they were leaving nature to herself. My thoughts gradually assumed a darker and more imposing complexion. The shadows of the night which were becoming every moment deeper, the vast silence which surrounded me and which was only broken by a very few, distant noises, induced a calmer and more solemn feeling after my imaginings. I scanned the greyish horizon though I could no longer discern where it began or ended, and for this very reason it gave me a sensation of boundlessness. I had experienced nothing of the sort for a long time: forever absorbed in personal reflections, my eyes always fixed on my own situation, I had become a stranger to any general notion; I had only been concerned with Ellénore who inspired in me only pity and weariness; with myself, for whom I no longer had any esteem. I had, so to speak, shrunk into a new kind of self-centred life, devoid of courage, full of discontent and humiliation. I was glad to become alive again to thoughts of a different order, and to find that I still had the faculty of forgetting myself and indulging in disinterested meditations; my mind seemed to be recovering from a long and shameful degradation.

Almost the whole of the night was spent in this way. I wandered at random; I crossed fields, woods and hamlets where everything was still. From time to time, through the darkness, a faint light from some distant dwelling caught my eye. And I said to myself: 'There, perhaps, some luckless man or woman is tossing in pain or struggling with death—that unaccountable mystery which, though an everyday occurrence, does not appear to be accepted by men as yet—that certain end which neither consoles nor calms us—a subject of habitual unconcern and of passing terror! And,' I reflected, 'I too am prone to this mad inconsequence! I rebel against life as if life will never end! I cause misery about me in order to recapture a few wretched years which time will soon snatch from me! Ah! let me rejoice in watching time pass and my days speed by one after another; let me remain unmoved, as an impassive observer of an existence which has already run half its course. Whether one seizes it or rends it to pieces, its length cannot be prolonged! Is it worth a struggle?'

The idea of death has always had a strong influence on me. It has always been sufficient to calm me immediately, even in my moments of keenest emotional excitement. It produced its usual effect on my mind; I became less bitterly disposed towards Ellénore. All my irritation disappeared; the impression that remained of this night of delirium was simply one of pleasantness, almost of tranquillity: the physical weariness which I felt may possibly have contributed to this peaceful state.

Day was returning. I could already distinguish objects. I perceived I was rather a long way from Ellénore's house. I imagined her anxiety, and, as fast as my tired limbs would go, I was hastening back to her when I met a man on horseback whom she had sent to look for me. He told me that for twelve hours she had been a prey to the liveliest fears. After going to Warsaw and scouring the countryside, she had returned home in a state of indescribable anguish and had dispatched the inhabitants of the village in all directions to look for me.

This account at first filled me with a rather bitter impatience. I was angered at finding myself subjected by Ellénore to this insufferable supervision. I repeatedly but vainly told myself that her love alone was the cause. Was not that very love the cause of all my misfortune? However, I managed to subdue this feeling which I considered reprehensible. I knew she must be alarmed and ill. I took a horse and swiftly covered the distance which separated us. She received me with transports of joy. I was moved at her emotion. We spoke little because it soon occurred to her that I must be in need of rest; I left her, this time at least, without having said anything to pain her heart.

VIII THE NEXT DAY I ROSE HAUNTED BY THE same ideas which had troubled me the previous day. And in the days that followed my unrest grew. Ellénore was unable to discover the cause: I answered her impetuous questions in constrained monosyllables; I steeled myself against her insistence, knowing as I did that frankness on my part would lead to her suffering, and that her suffering would force me to dissemble afresh.

Ellénore, uneasy and astonished, turned to one of her women friends in order to discover the secret she accused me of hiding; eager to deceive herself, she sought a fact where there was only a feeling. This friend spoke to me of my strange humour, of how carefully I rejected any idea of a lasting relationship, of my unexplainable thirst for breaking our ties and for seeking solitude. I listened to her for a long while in silence; I had hitherto told no one that I no longer loved Ellénore; I could not bring myself to make a confession which seemed to me an act of treachery. But I wanted to justify myself; I told my story with circumspection, praising Ellénore highly, admitting that I had been inconsiderate in my conduct but placing the responsibility on the difficulties of our situation. I did not utter a single word which would show clearly that the real difficulty was the absence of love on my part.

The woman who was listening was moved by my story: she saw generosity in what I called my weakness, misfortune in what I called my hardness. The same explanations which infuriated the passionate Ellénore carried conviction in the mind of her impartial friend. One is so just when one is disinterested! Whoever you are, never entrust to another the interests of your heart; the heart alone can plead its own cause; the heart alone can fathom its own wounds. Any third person becomes a judge, analysing and compromising; he is able to

conceive of indifference, to admit it as possible and recognize it as inevitable; for this very reason, he excuses
it and, much to his surprise, indifference appears as
legitimate.

Ellénore's reproaches had convinced me that I was
guilty; I learned from the person who was defending her
that I was merely unhappy. I was drawn into a complete avowal of my sentiments: I admitted that I felt
devotion, sympathy and pity for Ellénore, but added
that love had no place in my self-imposed duties. That
truth, till then locked in my heart and only occasionally
revealed to Ellénore in the heat of emotion and anger,
assumed in my eyes greater reality and power for the
simple reason that another person shared it. It is a great
step, an irreparable step, when one suddenly reveals to
a third person the hidden intricacies of an intimate
affair of the heart; the light which penetrates this
sanctuary picks out and completes the work of destruction which darkness had enveloped in its shades. Thus
it is that bodies shut in tombs often preserve their
original shape until the outside air reaches them and
reduces them to dust.

Ellénore's woman friend left me. I do not know
what account she gave of our conversation, but, as I
approached the drawing-room, I heard Ellénore speaking in very animated tones; when she saw me she became silent. Soon, in various forms, she produced general
ideas which were in reality particular attacks. She would
say, for example: 'Nothing is stranger than the zeal of
certain friends; there are people who enthusiastically
take up your interests the better to desert your cause;
they call this attachment: I would prefer hatred.' It was
easy for me to see that Ellénore's friend had taken my
side against her and had angered her by not appearing
to judge me sufficiently guilty. I felt I had a certain
secret understanding with another person against Ellénore: between our hearts this constituted yet another
barrier.

Several days later, Ellénore went further: she was
quite unable to exercise self-control; as soon as she
thought she had a subject for complaint, reckless and
unsparing, she would immediately seek an explanation,

preferring the danger of a breach to being forced to
dissemble. The two friends separated, having fallen
out for good.

'Why,' I asked Ellénore, 'why bring strangers into our
intimate disputes? Do we need a third party in order to
understand each other? And if we no longer understand
each other, what third party can remedy that?' 'You are
right,' she replied. 'But it is your fault; I never had to
appeal to others before in order to reach your heart.'

Suddenly, Ellénore announced her plan to change our
mode of life. I gathered from what she said that she
attributed the discontent which was devouring me to
the solitary fashion in which we were living. She was
exhausting all the wrong explanations before resigning
herself to the right one. We were spending monotonous
evenings, alone together in silence or ill-humour; the
spring of long conversations had run dry.

Ellénore decided to attract into her house the noble
families who lived in the neighbourhood or in Warsaw.
I could easily foresee the obstacles and dangers accompanying these attempts. Her relatives who were contend-
ing with her for her inheritance had revealed the errors
of her past and spread many slanderous rumours about
her. The thought of the humiliations she would be
facing made me shudder and I tried to dissuade her
from this enterprise. My remonstrances were unavailing;
I wounded her pride by my fears, even though I expressed them with circumspection. She supposed I was
uneasy on account of our relationship and because of
the equivocal nature of her life; she was all the more
anxious to recapture an honourable place in society,
nor were her efforts wholly unsuccessful.

The fortune which she enjoyed, her beauty which
time had as yet only slightly diminished, the very rumours about her life—everything about her excited
curiosity. She even found herself surrounded by a numerous society; but she was haunted by a secret feeling
of embarrassment and uneasiness. I was dissatisfied with
my situation and she imagined it was with hers. Rest-
lessly she tried to find a way out; urged on by the ardour
of her desire, she could not stop to plan; her false
position made her conduct incalculable and her steps

over-precipitate. Her judgment was sound, but narrow; its soundness was perverted by her passionate nature, and its narrowness prevented her from seeing which was the best course of action and from appreciating the finer points. For the first time, she had an aim; but in rushing towards it she missed it. What a number of humiliations she had to swallow without telling me of them! How many times I blushed for her without having the strength to tell her! The power which reserve and moderation have over men is such that I had seen her more respected by the friends of Count P—— as his mistress than she was by her neighbours as the heir to a great fortune, surrounded by her vassals. By turns lofty and imploring, considerate and susceptible, there was some violent spirit in her actions and in her words which destroyed the respect which only calm can inspire.

In picking out Ellénore's defects in this way, I am accusing and condemning myself. One word from me would have calmed her: why did I not pronounce it?

We were, however, living together more peacefully, being diverted from our usual run of thoughts by distractions. Except at intervals, we were not alone together; and as we had boundless mutual confidence on all matters save our personal feelings concerning one another, we replaced our feelings by observations and facts, and our conversations recovered a certain charm. But soon, this new mode of life became a source of fresh perplexity to me. Lost in the crowd surrounding Ellénore, I became aware of the fact that I was the object of astonishment and blame. The time was approaching when Ellénore's lawsuit was to be judged; her adversaries were claiming that she had alienated her father's affections by innumerable deviations from the path of virtue; my presence supported their assertions. Her friends reproached me with damaging her cause. They excused her passion for me, but accused me of lacking in tact. They said I was taking advantage of a sentiment which I should have moderated. I alone knew that, if I left her, she would have been drawn after me and, to follow me, she would have neglected paying any heed to her fortune or to the counsels of prudence. I could not confide this secret to the world; I therefore appeared in Ellénore's house as a stranger harmful to the success of the steps which were to decide her fate. By a strange reversal of facts, whilst I was the victim of her indomitable will, she was the one who was pitied as the victim of my ascendancy over her.

A new circumstance added a further complication to this painful situation.

A curious transformation suddenly occurred in Ellénore's behaviour and manners. Until this time, she had appeared to be solely concerned with me; all at once, I saw her receiving and seeking attention from the men surrounding her. This woman who was so reserved, so cold and distrustful, seemed suddenly to change her character. She was encouraging the sentiments and even the hopes of a crowd of young men; some of them were attracted by her beauty, and a few others, despite the errors of her past, were seriously aspiring to her hand in marriage. She granted them long private conversations, adopting towards them those ambiguous but attractive attitudes which gently reject merely to detain, since they betray indecision and deferment rather than indifference and refusal. Later she told me, and the facts go to prove the truth of her statement, that she was acting in this way through a pitiful miscalculation. She imagined she could revive my love by exciting my jealousy; but all she did was to stir ashes which nothing could rekindle. In this attempt there may also have been, without her realizing it, an element of feminine vanity! My coolness wounded her; she wanted to prove to herself that she still had the power to please. And, finally, perhaps she found in the waste in which I left her heart a sort of consolation in hearing words of love which I had long ceased to pronounce.

Be that as it may, for some while I was mistaken about her motives. I glimpsed the dawn of my coming liberty and rejoiced. Fearful lest I should interrupt by some false move this great crisis with which I thought my deliverance was bound up, I became more gently disposed and appeared happier. Ellénore mistook my gentleness for tenderness, and my hope to see her at last happy without me for the desire to make her happy. She congratulated herself on the success of her stratagem. Sometimes, however, she became alarmed at my freedom from uneasiness; she reproached me with not putting any obstacles in the path of her affairs which apparently threatened to make me lose her. I dismissed these accusations jokingly but did not always manage to calm her fears; her real character showed through the part she was forcing herself to play. The scenes began again, on other grounds, but equally stormy. Ellénore blamed me for her own faults, she intimated that a single word would make her completely mine again; then, offended at my silence, she once more plunged into flirtation with a sort of fury.

This is where, I feel, I shall be accused of weakness. I wanted to be free and I could have been with general approbation; perhaps I should have been, for Ellénore's conduct justified me and seemed to compel me to act. But did I not know that this conduct on her part was my work? Did I not know that Ellénore, at the bottom of her heart, had not ceased to love me? Could I punish her for an imprudence which I made her commit and, with cold hypocrisy, find a pretext in these imprudences to abandon her without pity?

Of course, I do not wish to make excuses for myself. I condemn myself more severely than perhaps another would in my place; but I can at least solemnly testify that I have never acted out of cold calculation and that I have always been guided by true and natural feelings. How is it that, with these feelings, I have, for so long, merely caused my own unhappiness and that of others?

Meanwhile, people in society were observing me with surprise. My stay with Ellénore could only be explained by a great attachment to her, yet my indifference concerning the bonds which she always seemed ready to contract belied this attachment. My unexplainable tolerance was attributed to a looseness of principles, to a heedlessness about morals which proclaimed, they said, a profoundly egotistic man whom the world had corrupted. These conjectures, which were so much the more likely to make an impression in that they were in keeping with the minds which conceived them, were generally adopted and repeated. They finally reached my ears and I was indignant at this unexpected discovery: as a

reward for my long services, I was misjudged and calum-
niated; on account of a woman, I had abandoned all
interests and rejected all the pleasures of life, and yet it
was I who was condemned!

I had a heated argument with Ellénore: she spoke the
word and this mob of admirers, whom she had summoned to make me fear I should lose her, vanished. She
restricted her society to a few women and a small
number of men advanced in years. Everything about us
resumed a regular appearance; but we were only the
more unhappy: Ellénore imagined she had new claims
on me; I was loaded with new chains.

I cannot describe what bitterness and rages were en-
gendered by this further complicating of our relationship. Our life was one perpetual storm; intimacy lost all
its charm and love all its sweetness; we no longer even
enjoyed those occasional returns to former happy states
which, for a few brief moments, seem to heal incurable
wounds. The truth broke out in every direction, and I
employed, to make myself understood, the harshest and
most pitiless expressions. I did not stop till I saw Ellénore in tears, and those very tears of hers, falling drop
by drop like burning lava on my heart, forced me to cry
out but could not drag a disavowal from me. It was then
that, more than once, I saw her rise, pale and prophetic:
'Adolphe!' she would say, 'you do not know the wrong
you are doing; you will learn one day, you will learn
it from me, when you have precipitated me into the
grave!' Miserable wretch that I am, why, when she was
speaking thus, did I not cast myself into the grave
before her?

IX I HAD NOT RETURNED TO BARON T——'S SINCE my first visit. One morning I received the following note from him:

'The advice I gave you did not merit so long an absence. Whatever decision you take in a matter which concerns you alone, you are none the less the son of my dearest friend. It will give me much pleasure to have your company and to introduce you to a circle which, I feel sure, you will find to your taste. May I add (without intending any condemnation) that the stranger your mode of life, the more important it is for you to dispel what are probably ill-founded prejudices by showing yourself in society.'

I was grateful for the kindness shown to me by an elderly man. I paid him a visit. Ellénore was not mentioned. The Baron kept me to dinner: that day there were only a few rather witty and agreeable men. At first, I was embarrassed, but I took myself in hand, revived my spirits and spoke; I displayed my wit and knowledge to the best of my ability. I perceived that I was winning admiration. This kind of success allowed me once more to enjoy self-esteem—a pleasure of which I had long since been deprived, and this pleasure made the society of Baron T—— more agreeable to me.

My visits became frequent. He entrusted me with some work in connection with his mission which he thought I could conveniently do. Ellénore was at first surprised at this revolution in my life; but I told her of the Baron's friendship for my father and of the pleasure I felt at being able to console the latter by appearing to busy myself with something useful. Poor Ellénore! (I am writing this now with a feeling of remorse.) She was happier, seeing me appear more peaceful, and resigned herself, without complaining too much, to spending the best part of the day separated from me. The Baron, on the other hand, when a little more

91

confidence was established between us, again spoke to
me of Ellénore. It was my positive intention always to
speak well of her, but, without realizing it, I expressed
myself in a freer and more off-hand fashion: either I
indicated by general maxims that I recognized the
necessity of breaking away from her, or else jokes came
to my aid; I spoke laughingly of women and of the
difficulty of breaking with them. These remarks used to
amuse an old minister with a well-worn heart, who
remembered vaguely that, in his youth, he had also been
harassed by love affairs. In this way, by the mere fact
that I had hidden my feelings, I more or less deceived
everyone; I was deceiving Ellénore, for I knew Baron
T—— wanted to separate me from her, and I said nothing to her of this; I was deceiving the Baron, for I let
him hope that I was ready to break my bonds. This
duplicity was far from my natural character, but man
becomes depraved as soon as he has in his heart a single
thought which he is constantly obliged to dissimulate.

Till then I had met at the Baron's house only the
men of his intimate circle. One day, he invited me to
stay for a big celebration which he was offering in honour of the birth of his master. He said to me: 'You will
meet there the prettiest women in Poland: it is true that
you will not find there the one you love; I am sorry, but
some women one only sees in their own homes.' This
remark affected me painfully; I kept silent but reproached myself inwardly at not taking Ellénore's defence, knowing that if anyone had attacked me in her
presence she would have defended me very vigorously.

It was a numerous gathering; people observed me
closely. I heard my father's name being whispered and
also that of Ellénore and Count P——. When I approached, they stopped talking and started again when
I moved away. They had demonstrated to me the fact
that they were telling my story and each person was no
doubt telling it after his own fashion; my situation was
intolerable; a cold sweat broke out on my forehead. I
blushed and turned pale by turns.

The Baron noticed my embarrassment. He came to
me and was even more attentive and kinder than usual;
he took every opportunity of praising me and, through

the great influence of his consideration, forced the others to show me the same attentions.

When everyone had withdrawn, Baron T—— said to me: 'I should like once more to speak to you frankly. Why let this situation from which you suffer continue? Whom are you benefiting? Do you think people do not know what goes on between you and Ellénore? Everyone is aware of your bitterness and your mutual discontent. You are doing yourself harm by your weakness and no less harm by your harshness; for, the crowning absurdity is that you are not giving happiness to the woman who makes you so unhappy.'

I was still wincing from the pain I had felt that evening. The Baron showed me several letters from my father. They displayed a far greater affliction than I had supposed. I was much disturbed. The idea that I was prolonging Ellénore's torment increased my indecision. Finally, as if everything was conspiring against her, whilst I was still hesitating, she herself by her impetuosity finished making up my mind. I had been away all day; the Baron had detained me after the gathering; the night was growing late. I was handed, in the presence of Baron T——, a letter from Ellénore. I saw in the Baron's eyes a sort of pity at my servitude. Ellénore's letter was full of bitterness. 'What!' I exclaimed to myself, 'can I not be free for one day? I cannot breathe one hour in peace. She pursues me everywhere, like a slave who must be brought back to her feet'; and, all the more violently because I felt I was weak, I cried: 'Yes, I will undertake to break with Ellénore, I shall not be afraid to tell her so myself, you can inform my father accordingly in advance.'

As I said these words, I hastened away from the Baron. The words I had just pronounced lay heavily on my conscience and I could scarcely believe the promise I had given.

Ellénore was impatiently waiting for me. By a strange coincidence, during my absence, some one had spoken to her for the first time of the efforts Baron T—— was making to separate us. She had been told of the remarks I had passed and the jokes I had made. Her suspicions being aroused, she had called to mind several circumstances which appeared to confirm them. My sudden intimacy with a man whom I had never been in the habit of seeing before, the close friendship between this man and my father, seemed to her irrefutable proof. Her anxiety had developed to such an extent in the course of a few hours that I found her fully convinced of what she called my treachery.

I had come to her, determined to make a clean breast of everything. But, being accused by her—who will believe it?—all I did was to evade every issue. I even denied, yes, I denied that day what I had decided to tell her the next.

It was late; I left her! I hurried to bed in order to bring that long day to a close; and when I was quite sure it was ended, I felt, for the time being, freed from an enormous weight.

The next day, I did not rise till about noon, as if, by delaying our interview, I had delayed the fatal moment. Ellénore had become reassured during the night through her own reflections and also through what I had said the previous evening. She spoke of her affairs with an air of confidence which showed only too clearly that she regarded our lives as indissolubly knit. Where could I find words which would cast her back into isolation?

Time was passing at an alarming rate. With each minute the need for an explanation grew. The second of the three days which I had named was already nearing its close. Baron T—— was expecting me at the latest on the following day. His letter to my father had gone and I was to break my promise without having made the slightest effort to fulfil it. I constantly went and came, took Ellénore's hand, began a sentence and immediately broke it off; I watched the sun sinking towards the horizon. Night came and I made a further postponement. I had one day left.

This day passed like the previous one. I wrote to Baron T—— to ask him for more time: and—a natural thing for weak characters to do—I filled my letter with countless reasons to justify this delay, to show that it in no wise altered the decision I had taken and that my ties with Ellénore could, as from that moment, be considered severed for ever.

X   I SPENT THE NEXT FEW DAYS IN A MORE PEACE-
ful frame of mind. I had relegated the necessity to act to some vague future date; it no
longer haunted me like a spectre; I imagined
I had plenty of time to prepare Ellénore for the blow.
I tried to be gentler and more tender with her in order
to preserve at least memories of friendship. My emotion
was quite different from anything I had known before.
I had beseeched heaven to raise suddenly between Ellénore and me an insurmountable barrier. That barrier
had suddenly appeared. I gazed at Ellénore as on a being
I was going to lose. Her exacting ways which had so
often appeared intolerable to me no longer dismayed
me, for I anticipated my release from them. While still
yielding to her, I felt freer and no longer subject to that
inner rebellion which formerly made me ever prone to
rend everything to pieces. I was no longer impatient; I
felt, on the contrary, a secret desire to put off the fatal
moment.

Ellénore noticed this more affectionate and responsive
disposition: she herself became less bitter. I sought the
intimate conversations I had avoided; I took pleasure in
her loving expressions which had formerly seemed so
importunate and now seemed precious as being each
time possibly the last.

One evening, we had parted after a conversation
which had been sweeter than usual. The secret I carried
in my breast made me sad; but there was no violence in
my sadness. The uncertainty in which I had sought to
wrap the date of our separation allowed me to brush the
idea aside. During the night, I heard an unusual noise
in the hall. It soon ceased and I attached no importance
to it. In the morning, however, it came back to my
mind; I wanted to know the cause of it and made my
way to Ellénore's bedroom. What was my astonishment
when I was told that for twelve hours she had been

suffering from a high fever, that a doctor who had been called by her servants had declared her life in danger, and that she had peremptorily forbidden my being warned or my going to her room!

I wanted to insist. The doctor himself came out to explain to me the necessity of causing her no excitement. Not being aware of the true reason, he attributed her order to the desire not to cause me any alarm. With anguish I questioned Ellénore's servants as to what could have plunged her so suddenly into so dangerous a state. She had received, after our parting the previous evening, a letter from Warsaw brought by a man on horseback; having opened it and scanned the contents, she fainted; on coming to, she had thrown herself on to her bed without a word. One of her women, alarmed at the state in which Ellénore seemed to be, stayed in her room without her knowledge. In the middle of the night, this woman saw her seized by so violent a fit of trembling that it shook the bed on which she was lying: the woman wanted to call me but Ellénore opposed this with such vehemence that she had not dared disobey. A doctor was sent for; Ellénore had refused and was still refusing to answer his questions; she had spent the night uttering incoherent words which they had not been able to understand, and often pressing her handkerchief over her mouth as if to prevent herself speaking.

Whilst I was listening to these details another woman who had been staying beside Ellénore ran up to us in great alarm. Ellénore appeared to have lost the use of her senses. She could not recognize any objects around her. She was uttering cries and calling out my name; then, terrified, she would make a sign with her hand as if she wanted something to be taken away which was hateful to her.

I entered her room. I saw at the foot of her bed two letters. One was mine to Baron T——, the other was from the Baron to Ellénore. I now saw only too clearly what lay behind the mystery. All my efforts to obtain more time to devote to our last farewells had thus been turned against the unhappy woman whom I had sought to spare. Ellénore had read in my own handwriting my promises to abandon her, promises dictated by my desire to stay longer beside her and which the very keenness of this desire had made me repeat with countless variations. The impartial eye of Baron T—— had easily detected in these protestations, reiterated in every line, the lack of resolution which I was disguising and the ruses of my own hesitation; but this cruel man had calculated all too clearly that Ellénore would only see in them an irrevocable sentence. I went to her: she looked at me without recognizing me. I spoke to her: she shuddered. 'What is that sound?' she cried. 'It is the voice which hurt me.' The doctor remarked that my presence added to her delirium and begged me to go away. How can I describe what I felt during three long hours? At last, the doctor came out. Ellénore had fallen into a heavy slumber. He did not despair of saving her life if, when she awoke, the fever had abated.

Ellénore slept a long while. When I was told of her awakening, I wrote to her to ask her to receive me. She invited me to enter. I wanted to speak; she interrupted me. 'Let me hear no cruel word from you,' she said. 'I make no further demands. I oppose nothing; but that voice I loved so much, that voice which moved my heart, do not, I pray, let it penetrate to my heart to rend it. Adolphe, Adolphe, I was violent and perhaps I offended you; but you do not know what I have suffered. Please God you never do!'

She became greatly agitated. She rested her forehead on my hand; it was burning; a terrible convulsion contorted her features. 'My dear Ellénore!' I cried. 'In heaven's name, listen to me. Yes, I am guilty: that letter——.' She shuddered and tried to move away. I held her and continued: 'I am weak and restless and I may have yielded to a cruel pressure; but, have you not a thousand proofs that I am unable to wish for anything to separate us? I have been discontented, unhappy and unjust; perhaps, by your struggling too violently against a rebellious imagination, you have given greater force to passing impulses which I now despise; but can you doubt my deep affection for you? Are not our souls bound together by a thousand bonds which noth-

ing can break? Have we not shared all the past? Can
we look back at these last years without recalling the
impressions we shared, the pleasures we enjoyed and
the pains we bore together? Ellénore, let us this day
begin a fresh life, remembering our hours of happiness
and love.'

She looked at me doubtfully for some time. Then
she said: 'But your father, well, your duties, your
family and what is expected of you——.'

'Oh, I suppose, some time,' I replied. 'One day
perhaps——.'

She noticed I hesitated and cried: 'Oh, why did he
give me back hope only to snatch it away from me
immediately? Adolphe, I thank you for your efforts:
they have helped me, they have helped me so much
the more in that they will, I trust, require no sacrifice
from you; but, I beg you, do not let us speak any more
of the future——. You need not reproach yourself with
anything, whatever happens. You have been good to
me. I wanted what was impossible. Love was all my
life: it could not be all yours. Now, care for me a
few days more.' Tears streamed from her eyes; her
breath came more freely; she leaned her head on my
shoulder. 'This,' she said, 'is where I always wanted
to die.'

I pressed her to my heart, I again abjured my plans
and disclaimed my cruel rages. 'No,' she went on, 'you
must be free and contented.' 'How can I if you are
unhappy?' 'I shall not be unhappy for long; you will
not have to pity me for long.' I would not entertain
fears which were, I hoped, chimerical. 'No, no, my
dear Adolphe,' she said. 'When you have called on
death for a long while, heaven finally sends you some
infallible presentiment, telling you your prayer is
answered.' I swore I would never leave her. 'I always
hoped so and now I am sure of it.'

It was one of those winter days when the sun seems
to light the greyish countryside with a melancholy
light, as if it looked pityingly on the earth which it
has ceased to warm. Ellénore suggested going out. 'It
is cold,' I said. 'No matter, I would like to go for a
walk with you.' She took my arm; we wandered a long

time in silence; she was walking with difficulty and leaning almost entirely on me. 'Let us stop a moment.' 'No,' she replied. 'I like to feel I am still supported by you.' We relapsed into silence. The sky was calm; but the trees were leafless; no breeze stirred the air, no bird flew through it: everything was motionless and the only sound to be heard was that of the frozen grass crunching under our feet.

'How calm everything is!' Ellénore said. 'How resigned nature is! The heart should perhaps also learn resignation.' She sat on a stone; suddenly she knelt and bowed her head into her two hands. I heard her murmur a few words. I preceived she was praying. Finally, she rose and said: 'Let us go home, the cold has chilled me. I am afraid I may faint. Say nothing; I am not in a state to follow what you say.'

From this day on, I watched Ellénore weaken and waste away. I called in doctors from all parts to see her: some declared she was suffering from an incurable disease whilst others deluded me with vain hopes; but, with an invisible hand, sombre nature continued her remorseless work in silence. At times, Ellénore seemed to be returning to life, as if the iron hand which weighed on her had been withdrawn. She would raise her languid head; more colour would come into her cheeks; her eyes became lighter; but, suddenly, in this cruel game of a mysterious power, the deceptive improvement would disappear without the doctor's art being able to discover the cause. I saw her thus advancing by degrees to destruction. I saw the warning signs of death being engraved on her face and I witnessed the humiliating and lamentable spectacle of this energetic and proud character being subjected by physical suffering to a thousand confused and incoherent strains, as if, in these terrible moments, the mind oppressed by the body, was being transformed in every way, the more easily to submit to the degeneration of the organs.

One sentiment never varied in Ellénore's heart: her tenderness for me. Her weak state rarely allowed her to speak; but she gazed at me in silence and her eyes seemed to be asking me for life—life which I could no longer give her. I feared causing her any violent emotion; I invented excuses to go out and wandered over all the places I had visited with her; I watered with my tears the stones, the roots of the trees, every object which recalled her to me.

It was not that I was mourning my love, it was a darker, sadder feeling; love identifies itself so completely with the loved one that there is some charm even in despair. It struggles against reality, against destiny; the fervour of desire misleads it as to its strength and exalts it in the midst of suffering. Mine was gloomy and solitary; I did not hope to die with Ellénore; I was going to live without her in this desert of a world which I had so often wished to cross independently. I had broken the being I loved; I had broken that companion heart to mine which, in its indefatigable tenderness, had persisted in devoting itself to me; I was already being immured in solitude. Ellénore was still breathing, but I could not confide my thoughts to her; I was already alone on this earth. No longer could I live in that atmosphere of love which she created around me; the air I breathed seemed harsher, the faces of men I met more indifferent to me; all nature seemed to tell me I would now cease to be loved for ever.

Ellénore's danger became suddenly more imminent; unmistakable symptoms announced that the end was at hand: a priest of her faith informed her of this. She asked me to bring her a casket containing many papers; she had a few burned before her, but seemed to be looking for one which she could not find, and for which she showed great anxiety. I begged her to stop searching as this upset her. She had twice fainted during the search. 'I agree, my dear Adolphe,' she said, 'but grant me one thing. You will find amongst my papers, somewhere, a letter addressed to you; burn it without reading it, I implore you to do this in the name of our love, in the name of these my last moments which you have made easier.' I promised and she was content. 'Now,' she said, 'let me devote myself to my religious duties; I have many sins to expiate: my love for you was perhaps a sin; I should not believe that, however, if my love had made you happy.'

I left her: I did not return until all her people went in to take part in the last solemn prayers. On my knees in a corner of her room, I was at times sunk in my thoughts, at others observing with a sort of unintentional curiosity all those men who had gathered there, the terror of some, the wandering thoughts of others, and the peculiar effect of habit which introduces indifference into all prescribed forms and causes the most solemn and awe-inspiring ceremonies to be considered merely as matters of convention. I heard men repeating the funeral words mechanically, as if they would never be the principal actors in a similar scene, as if one day they would not themselves have to die. I was, however, far from scorning these practices; is there a single one of them which man in his ignorance would dare declare useless? They brought calm to Ellénore; they helped her to cross that terrible strait to which we are all progressing, though not one of us can foresee what he will then experience. I am not surprised that man needs a religion; what astonishes me is that he should ever think himself sufficiently strong or sufficiently secure against misfortune to dare reject one: his weakness should, I feel, dispose him to invoke them all; in the dark night which surrounds us, can we afford to reject a single gleam? In the midst of the stream which is bearing us away, is there a single branch to which we dare refuse to cling?

The deep impression which this lugubrious solemnity had produced on Ellénore seemed to have tired her. She fell into a rather peaceful sleep, and awakened in less pain; I was alone in her room and we spoke at long intervals. The doctor who had shown the greatest perspicacity in his conjectures had told me that she would not live more than twenty-four hours. I looked in turn at a clock which told me the time and at Ellénore's face on which I could detect no new change. Each minute which passed revived my hopes, and I called into question the auguries of a fallacious art. Suddenly, Ellénore sprang up; I caught her in my arms. Her whole body was seized by convulsions; her eyes sought mine, but an obscure terror was depicted in them; she seemed to be trying to beg mercy of some threatening object which was hidden from sight; she raised herself and fell back several times. One could see she was trying to flee; it was as if she was struggling against an invisible physical power, which, tired of waiting for the fatal moment, had seized her and was holding her by force on to this deathbed in order to dispatch her. She yielded at last to the relentlessness of hostile nature; as her limbs gave way, she seemed to recover consciousness; she pressed my hand and made as if to weep, but there were no tears; she wanted to speak, there was no more voice. As if resigned, she let her head fall on the arm on which she was leaning; her breathing became slower; a few moments later she was no more.

I remained motionless for a long while beside the lifeless Ellénore. The conviction that she was dead had not yet penetrated to my mind; my eyes gazed in stunned surprise at this inanimate body. One of her women who had entered spread the sinister news throughout the house. The noise about me aroused me from the lethargy into which I had sunk; I rose; it was then that I felt the rending pain and all the horror of the final parting. All that bustle and activity of vulgar life, all those attentions and that excitement which no longer concerned her, dispelled the illusion which I was prolonging, that illusion which allowed me to believe I still existed with Ellénore. I felt the last link break and hideous reality come for ever between us. How heavily this liberty weighed upon me which I had so often regretted! How much my heart missed that dependence against which I had often rebelled! Formerly, all my actions had an aim; I was sure that each one would either spare a pain or cause a pleasure; of this I had complained; I had been irritated that a friendly eye should observe my movements, that the happiness of another should be attached to them. No one now observed them; they interested nobody; no one contended with me for my time nor my hours; no voice called me back when I went out. I was free indeed; I was no longer loved. I was a stranger to all the world.

All Ellénore's papers were brought to me as she had ordered; in every line, I found fresh proof of her love, new sacrifices she had made for me and hidden from me. At last, I found the letter I had promised to burn; I did not recognize it at first: it was without an address and unsealed. A few words caught my eye despite myself; I tried in vain to look away, I could not resist the desire to read the whole of the letter. I scarcely have the strength to copy it: Ellénore had written it after one of those violent scenes prior to her malady. 'Adolphe,' she said to me, 'why are you so relentless with me? What is my crime? Loving you and not being able to exist without you. What strange pity makes you afraid to break a bond which is burdensome to you and makes you rend the heart of the unhappy person with whom you continue to stay on account of your pity? Why refuse me the poor pleasure of believing you at least generous? Why show yourself furious and weak? The idea of my suffering haunts you and the sight of that suffering is not sufficient to stop you! What do you demand? That I should leave you? Do you not see I have not the strength? Ah! it is you who do not love me, it is you who must find the strength in that heart of yours which is tired of me and which so much love cannot disarm. But you will not give me that strength, you will make me languish in tears, you will make me die at your feet.'

In another place she wrote: 'Tell me, is there a country in the world where I would not follow you? Is there a corner where I would not hide to live near you without being a burden to you? But no, you want no such thing. Everything I timidly and fearfully suggest—for you have chilled me with fear—you impatiently reject. The best I obtain is your silence. Such harshness is not in keeping with your character. You are kind; your actions are good and faithful: but what actions could efface your words? Those words, as cold and sharp as steel, resound about me: I hear them in the night; they pursue me, they pierce me, they spoil everything you do. Must I then die, Adolphe?

Well, you shall be satisfied; she will die, that poor creature whom you protected but whom you strike again
and again. She will die, that importunate Ellénore
whose presence you cannot bear, whom you consider
as an obstacle, for whom you can find no place in the
world where she would not weary you; she will die:
you will walk alone in the crowd which you are impatient to join! You shall know those men to whom
you are grateful now for their unconcern; and, perhaps,
one day, wounded by those arid hearts, you will regret
that soul who was yours, who lived by your affection,
who would have braved any dangers in your defence,
and whom you no longer deign to reward with a glance.'

Letter to the Publisher

Sir,

I am returning to you the manuscript which you were good enough to entrust to me. I thank you for this kindness; though, I must admit, it revived some sad memories which time had obliterated. I knew most of the people who figure in this story, for it is all too true. I often used to see the strange and unhappy Adolphe who is both the author and the hero; the charming Ellénore was worth a kinder fate and a more faithful heart, and I tried to save her by my counsels from the malefactor who was no less wretched than she, but who held her under a sort of spell and broke her heart by his weakness. Alas! the last time I saw her, I thought I had given her some support and steeled her mind against her heart. After too long an absence, I returned to the parts where I had left her and found only a tomb.

You should publish this anecdote, sir. It can hurt no one now and would, I think, serve a useful purpose. Ellénore's misfortune proves that even the most passionate feeling cannot afford to run counter to the existing order of things. Society is too powerful, it manifests itself in too many ways; it stirs too much bitterness into the love it has not sanctioned; it encourages those maladies of the mind: the leaning towards inconstancy, the impatience and the fatigue which at times suddenly seize the mind in the midst of love. People not directly concerned are astonishingly prone to be mischievous in the name of morality and harmful out of righteousness. It is as if the sight of affection

105

in others is disagreeable to them because they are incapable of it; and when they can avail themselves of some excuse, they take great pleasure in attacking and destroying it. Woe betide the woman whose happiness is founded on a sentiment which all unite to envenom; to fight against this sentiment, society (when not forced to recognize it as legitimate) arms itself with all that is bad in the heart of man in order to discourage all that is good!

Adolphe's example will not be less instructive if you add that, after having spurned the being who loved him, he was not less uneasy in mind, less agitated, nor less dissatisfied; that he made no use of the liberty he had reconquered at the cost of so much suffering and so many tears; and that, though he made himself truly blameworthy he also came to deserve pity.

If you need proof, sir, read these letters which will enlighten you as to Adolphe's fate; you will see him in many and varied circumstances, but always the victim of that mixture in his character of the self-centred and the soft-hearted which combined in him to produce his own unhappiness and that of others; seeing the evil consequences of an act before performing it, and retreating in despair having committed it; punished for his qualities more than for his defects, because his qualities were inspired by his emotions and not by his principles; in turn, the most devoted and the harshest of men, but since he always finished by being harsh after beginning by being devoted, he only left impressions of the wrongs he did.

The Publisher's Reply

Sir,
Yes, I will publish the manuscript which you sent back to me (not that I am of the same opinion as you as regards its possible usefulness; no one learns anything in this world save at his own expense, and the women who read it will all imagine they have met better men

than Adolphe or are themselves better than Ellénore);
but I shall publish it as a story showing with some truth
the misery of the human heart. If it contains an instructive lesson it is to men that the lesson applies: it
proves that this mind of which we are so proud helps
neither to find nor to give happiness; it proves that
character, firmness, faithfulness and kindness are gifts
one must pray for, and when I say kindness I do not
mean that fleeting pity which does not subdue impatience and does not prevent it from opening wounds
which a moment of regret had closed. The great question in life is the pain one causes and the most ingenious metaphysics cannot justify a man who has
broken the heart which loved him. What is more, I
hate the fatuity of a mind which fancies it excuses what
it explains; I hate the vanity which is only concerned
with itself when recounting the evil it has done, which
seeks to inspire pity in describing itself and which,
being indestructible, hovers over the ruins only to
analyse itself instead of to repent. I hate the weakness
which always blames others for its own impotence and
does not see that the evil is not in its surroundings
but in itself.

I should have guessed that Adolphe would be punished for his character by his character, that he would
follow no set road, fill no useful post, waste his faculties
with no other control than that of caprice, with no
other force than that of irritation; I should have
guessed all that, as I said, even if you had not sent me
new details concerning his subsequent life. I cannot
yet say whether I shall make use of them. Circumstances are of little importance, character is everything;
breaking with objects and other beings is of no avail—
you cannot break with yourself. You can change your
situation; but into each situation you carry the torment
from which you had hoped to rid yourself; and, as you
do not mend your ways when changing scenes, you
discover that you have merely added remorse to regrets
and sins to suffering.

THE RED NOTEBOOK

TRANSLATED FROM THE FRENCH

BY

NORMAN CAMERON

MY LIFE (1767-1787)

I

I WAS BORN on the 25th of October, 1767, at Lausanne, in Switzerland. My mother was Henriette de Chandieu, daughter of an old French family that had taken refuge from religious persecution in the canton of Vaud; and my father was Juste Constant de Rebecque, colonel of a Swiss regiment in the service of Holland. My mother died in childbed a week after my birth.

The first tutor of whom I retain any distinct memory was a German named Roelin, who used to thrash me and then smother me with caresses so that I should not complain to my father. I always faithfully kept my word to him, but nevertheless the thing was discovered, and the tutor was expelled from the house.

This man had conceived the rather ingenious idea of teaching me Greek by making me invent it for myself. That is to say, he proposed to me that we should together make a language to be used only by ourselves. I took a passionate interest in this idea. We first created an alphabet, into which he introduced Greek letters. Then we began a Dictionary, in which each French word was translated into a Greek one. All this remained in my head marvellously well, since I believed I was its inventor. I already knew a heap of Greek words, and was busy forming general rules for these words of my own creation—that is to say, I was learning Greek grammar—when the tutor was dismissed. I was then five years old.

When I was seven, my father took me to Brussels, where he intended to take charge of my education himself. He soon abandoned this project, and gave me as instructor a Frenchman, M. de La Grange, who was a surgeon-major in my father's regiment. This M. de La Grange professed himself an atheist. In other respects he was, as far as I can remember, a somewhat

111

mediocre man, very ignorant and excessively vain. He sought to seduce the daughter of a music-master at whose house I was taking lessons, and had several rather scandalous adventures. Finally he took lodgings for us in a house of doubtful reputation, to avoid interference with his pleasures. My father arrived from his regiment in a rage, and M. de La Grange was dismissed.

Until I should have another mentor, my father sent me as a boarder to my music-master. I lived in his house for several months. The family, which the father's talent had raised from the most humble class, fed me and cared for me very well, but could do nothing for my education. I had a few instructors, from whose lessons I played truant, and I had the use of a library in a neighbouring house that contained all the novels imaginable, as well as all the anti-religious works that were then in fashion. For eight or ten hours a day I read everything that came to hand, from the works of La Mettrie to the novels of Crébillon. My brains and my eyesight have suffered from it all my life.

My father, who from time to time came to see me, met an ex-Jesuit, who offered to take charge of me. Nothing came of this, I know not why. But about the same time a French ex-lawyer, who had left his country for rather pressing reasons, and was in Brussels with a wench whom he passed off as his housekeeper, was seeking to open an educational establishment. He offered his services, and was so plausible that my father believed he had discovered the very man. M. Gobert agreed, for a stiff price, to take me into his house. He gave me lessons only in Latin, of which he knew little, and history, which he taught me with the sole purpose of making me copy out a work which he had composed on this subject, and of which he wished to have several copies. But his handwriting was so bad, and my inattentiveness so great, that the copy had repeatedly to be begun anew, and during more than a year's work on it I never got further than the preface.

Finally, however, M. Gobert and his mistress became the subject of public gossip, and my father was informed of this. Thereupon, after scenes to which I was a witness, I left this third teacher, convinced for the third time that all those who were charged with my instruction and correction were themselves highly ignorant and immoral.

My father took me back to Switzerland, where I spent some time under his sole supervision, on his country estate. One of his friends mentioned to him a Frenchman of a certain age who lived in retirement at La Chaux-de-Fonds near Neuchâtel and had a reputation for intelligence and learning. My father made inquiries, from which it emerged that M. Duplessis—such was the Frenchman's name—was a defrocked monk who had escaped from his monastery, had changed his religion and was hiding himself, even in Switzerland, from persecution by France.

Although this information was not very favourable, my father sent for M. Duplessis, who proved to be better than his reputation. He thus became my fourth teacher. He was a man of very weak character, but kindly and intelligent. My father immediately took a great contempt for him, which he did not conceal from me: a rather bad preparation for the relationship between master and pupil. M. Duplessis discharged his duties to the best of his ability, and I made fair progress. I spent more than a year with him, either in Switzerland or at Brussels or in Holland. At the end of this period my father became completely dissatisfied with this tutor, and formed the design of sending me to an English university.

M. Duplessis left us to be tutor to a young Comte d'Aumale. Unfortunately, this young man had a sister who was rather pretty, and very light in her conduct. She amused herself by turning the head of the poor monk, who fell passionately in love with her. He concealed his love, because his condition, his fifty years and his appearance allowed him little hope, until he discovered that a wigmaker, less old and less ugly than himself, was more fortunate. He committed a thousand acts of folly, which were punished with pitiless severity, completely lost his head and ended by blowing out his brains.

Meanwhile my father had departed with me to

England, where, after a very brief stay in London, he took me to Oxford. He soon perceived that this university, to which the English do not go to complete their studies until they are twenty, was not suitable for a child of thirteen. He confined himself therefore to having me taught English, and to making some excursions in the neighbourhood for his own amusement. After two months we returned home with a young Englishman who had been recommended to my father as a suitable person to give me lessons without having the title or pretensions of a tutor: things of which my father, after four successive experiences, now had a horror. But the fifth experiment was like the previous ones: almost as soon as Mr. May had started travelling with us, my father found him ridiculous and insupportable. He confided his impressions to me, with the result that my new comrade was to me thereafter only an object of mockery and continual derision.

Mr. May spent a year and a half with us, in Switzerland and in Holland. We lived for a considerable while in the little town of Geertruydenberg. Here I fell in love, for the first time, with the daughter of the local commandant, an elderly officer who was a friend of my father. All day long I wrote long letters to her, which I never sent. I left the town without having declared my passion, which survived my departure by fully two months.

I have seen her since; and the idea that I had been in love with her had left her with an interest in—or perhaps merely a rather lively curiosity concerning—my subsequent doings. On one occasion she felt an impulse to question me about my sentiments towards her; but we were interrupted. Shortly after this she married, and died in childbed.

My father, whose dearest wish was to get rid of Mr. May, took the first opportunity of sending him back to England. We returned to Switzerland, where my father chose, for the purpose of giving me a few lessons, a M. Bridel, a man of some learning but very pedantic and heavy. My father was soon shocked by the self-importance, familiarity and bad manners of the new mentor he had selected for me. Becoming disgusted, after so many useless attempts, with the whole idea of domestic education, he decided to send me, at the age of fourteen, to a German university.

The Margravine of Anspach, who was in Switzerland at the time, directed his choice to Erlangen. My father took me there, and himself presented me at the little Court of the Margravine of Bareith, who was in residence there. She received us with all the cordiality that princes whose time is heavy on their hands feel towards strangers who amuse them, and conceived a great friendship towards me. Indeed, since I said whatever came into my head, thought everybody ridiculous and maintained with some adroitness the most distorted opinions, I must have been a fairly diverting person in a German Court. I also won the favour of the Margrave of Anspach, who gave me a post at his Court, which I visited to play faro and incur debts: these my father was foolish and kind enough to pay.

During my first year at this university I worked hard at my studies, but I also committed a thousand extravagances. The old Margravine invariably forgave me, and liked me all the better for them; and in this little town my favour at Court silenced all those who judged me more severely.

I wished, however, to win the glory of having a mistress. I chose a wench of rather bad reputation, whose mother had been guilty, on I know not what occasion, of I know not what impertinences towards the Margravine. The strange thing about this affair was that, on the one hand, I did not love the wench, and, on the other hand, she never gave herself to me. I am probably the only man whom she ever resisted. But the pleasure of creating and hearing the report that I was keeping a mistress consoled me both for spending my time with a person whom I did not love, and for not possessing the person whom I was keeping.

The Margravine was highly offended at this liaison, to which her remonstrations made me adhere all the more. These remonstrations served my purpose, which was that I should be talked about. At the same time the mother of my pretended mistress, still filled with hatred of the Margravine and flattered by the species of rivalry that had arisen between a princess and her daughter, never ceased urging me on to all sorts of behaviour offensive to the Court. Finally the Margravine lost patience, and forbade me to appear in the palace. I was at first much afflicted by my disgrace, and endeavoured to regain the favour that I had been at pains to lose. All those whom this favour had prevented from speaking ill of me now took their revenge. I became the object of general indignation and blame.

Anger and embarrassment drove me to commit still further follies. Finally my father, informed by the Margravine of all that was happening, ordered me to rejoin him at Brussels, and we departed together for Edinburgh. We arrived at this city on the 8th of July, 1782. My father had old acquaintances here, who received us with all the cordial friendship and hospitality that characterize the Scottish nation. I was placed with a professor of medicine who took in boarders.

My father remained in Scotland only three weeks. After his departure I applied myself to my studies with great fervour; and now began the most agreeable year of my life. Work was fashionable amongst the young people of Edinburgh. They had formed several literary and philosophic clubs. I belonged to some of these, and won distinction as a writer and orator, although in a foreign language. I established close relations with men who, for the most part, became well known in later years. Amongst these were Mackintosh, who is at present an important judge at Bombay; Laing, one of the best successors to Robertson, etc.

Amongst all these young people the one who seemed most promising was the son of a tobacconist, by name John Wilde. He had an almost absolute authority over all friends, although most of these were much his superiors in birth and fortune. His learning was immense, his zeal for study indefatigable, his conversation brilliant, his character excellent. After achieving a professorship by sheer merit, and publishing a book which most advantageously founded his reputation, he went raging mad, and is now either dead or chained in a cell on a bed of straw. Unhappy human race, what comes of us and of our hopes!

I lived for about eighteen months in Edinburgh, with great enjoyment and sufficient occupation, earning nothing but praise. Misfortune, however, would have it that a little Italian who gave me music lessons should introduce me to a faro bank kept by his brother. I played, I lost, I made debts right and left, and my whole sojourn in Edinburgh was spoilt.

At the time appointed by my father for my departure, I set off from the city promising my creditors that I would pay them, but leaving some of them highly displeased and having created some very unfavourable impressions. I travelled by London, where I spent three useless weeks, and arrived at Paris in March, 1785.

My father had made an arrangement for me which would have procured me all kinds of advantages, had I had the knowledge and wish to profit by them. I was to lodge with M. Suard, whose home was the meeting-place of a great number of men of letters, and who had promised to introduce me into the best Parisian society. Since my apartment was not ready, however, I at first put up at a lodging-house. Here I met an Englishman who was very rich and dissolute. I sought to imitate him in his follies, and had not been a month at Paris before I was over my head in debt. This was certainly, to some extent, the fault of my father, who had sent me at the age of eighteen, relying solely on my character, to a place where I could not fail to commit error after error.

Finally, however, I went to lodge with M. Suard, and my conduct became less extravagant. But the embarrassment into which I had plunged myself at the beginning had consequences that affected my entire stay in Paris. To crown my misfortune, my father felt obliged to put me under some kind of supervision, and for this purpose applied to a Protestant minister, the chaplain to the Dutch ambassador. The chaplain believed that he was performing an excellent act in recommending to my father a certain Baumier, who had been introduced to him as a Protestant persecuted by his family for religious reasons. This Baumier was a man of abandoned character, without fortune and without permanent place of abode, a true knight of fortune of the worst description. He set himself to gain a hold over me by half accommodating himself to all the follies that I wished to commit; and it was not his fault that I did not adopt the most dissolute and abject way of life. Since, apart from all his vices, he was without intelligence, very tedious and most insolent, I soon tired of a man who did nothing but accompany me on visits to wenches, and borrow money from me: so we quarrelled. He wrote, I suspect, to my father, and I suppose he exaggerated the ill account he gave of me, although the truth would have been entirely sufficient.

My father arrived at Paris in person, and took me off to Brussels, where he left me to return to his regiment. I stayed at Brussels from August until the end of November, sharing my time between the houses of Anet and Aremberg, old acquaintances of my father, who as such received me with great kindness, and a coterie of Genevans, which was more obscure but which I began to find much more agreeable.

In this coterie there was a woman of about twenty-six or twenty-eight, of very attractive appearance and most distinguished intelligence. I felt drawn towards her, without clearly admitting it to myself, for the reason that, by a few words that at first surprised me more than they delighted me, she allowed me to discover that she loved me. As I write, twenty-five years have elapsed since I made this discovery, and I still feel grateful as I recall the pleasure that it gave me.

Madame Johannot—such was her name—is set apart in my memory from all the other women I have known. My liaison with her was very brief, and proved to be no great thing. But she never made me pay for the sweetness she gave me with any admixture of agitation or grief; and at forty-four I still gratefully acknowledge the happiness that I owed to her when I was eighteen.

The poor woman came to a very sad end. Married to a man of despicable character and the most corrupt morals, she was first of all dragged off by him to Paris. Here he entered the service of the Party in power; became, although a foreigner, a member of the Convention; condemned the King to death; and continued, until the end of this all too famous assembly, to play a base and equivocal part. He soon relegated her to a village in Alsace, to make room for a mistress whom he kept in his own house. Finally he recalled her to Paris to live with the mistress, to whom he sought to compel her to act as servant. The ill-treatment that he showered upon her drove her to take poison. I was myself in Paris at the time, and was living in her neighbourhood. But I did not know that she was there, and she died within a few paces of a man whom she had loved, and who has never been able to pronounce her name without the deepest emotion. She died believing herself forgotten and forsaken by the whole world.

I had scarcely enjoyed her love for a month, when my father came to take me back to Switzerland. On my departure Madame Johannot and I exchanged sad and tender letters. She gave me an address at which she permitted me to continue writing to her; but she did not reply. I consoled myself without forgetting her; and it will be seen that other objects soon took her place. I saw her two years later at Paris, on a single occasion, a few years before her misfortunes. My liking for her revived, and I paid her a second visit. But she was gone: when I was told this, I felt an emotion of quite extraordinary sadness and violence. It was a sort of baleful presentiment, which her lamentable end has too well justified.

On my return to Switzerland I again spent some time in the country, studying by fits and starts and occupying myself with a work for which the first idea had come to me at Brussels, and which has never ceased to have a great attraction for me: it was to be a history of polytheism. I had at that time none of the knowledge that could enable me to write four passable lines on such a subject. Fed on the principles of eighteenth-century philosophy, and especially the works of Helvetius, my only thought was to make my contribution towards the destruction of what I called 'prejudices'. I had appropriated for my own use an assertion by the author of the *Esprit,* that paganism is much preferable to Christianity; and I sought to support this as-

sertion, to which I had given neither depth nor
scrutiny, with a few haphazard facts and a deal of epigrams and ranting statements that I believed to be
new.

Had I been less idle and less the prey of each new
impression, I would perhaps in two years have com-
pleted a very bad book, which would have won me a
small, ephemeral reputation. I would have been highly
pleased with this. Once committed by vanity, I would
not have been able to alter my opinion; and the first
paradox thus adopted would have held me in chains
all my life. If idleness has its drawbacks, it also has its
advantages.

I did not for long confine myself to a peaceful, stu-
dious life. A new love-affair came to distract me; and,
since I was three years older than I had been at Erlangen, I also committed three times as many acts of
folly. The object of my passion was an Englishwoman,
of about thirty to thirty-five, the wife of the English
ambassador at Turin. She had been very beautiful, and
still had pretty eyes, superb teeth and a charming
smile. Her house was most agreeable. There was much
gaming there, so that I was able to satisfy an inclination even keener than that which the lady herself inspired in me.

Mrs. Trevor was a great coquet, and had the sort
of dainty and precious wit that coquetry gives to
women who have no other. She was on rather bad
terms with her husband, from whom she was almost
permanently separated, and there were always five or
six young Englishmen in her train. I first thrust myself into her circle because it was more brilliant and
lively than any other in Lausanne. Later, seeing that
most of the young people in her entourage made love
to her, I took it into my head to win her favour. I
wrote her an eloquent letter, in which I declared my
passion for her. I handed her this letter one evening,
and returned the following morning for her answer.
Agitation due to uncertainty about the result of my
overture had put me in a kind of fever, which well
enough resembled the passion which at first I had
only sought to feign. Madame Trevor replied to me

in writing, as the circumstances demanded. She spoke of her obligations, and offered me the tenderest friendship. I should not have been halted by this expression, but should have seen to what such a friendship would have led us. Instead of this, I thought that the adroit thing to do was to indicate the most violent despair because she offered me only friendship in return for my love.

The poor woman, who had probably hitherto had to do with men of more experience, did not know how to act in this scene, which was the more embarrassing for her because I made no movement that might have put her in a position to terminate it in a manner agreeable to us both. I kept myself at ten paces' distance, and whenever she approached to calm or console me I retreated, repeating that, since all she had for me was friendship, there was nothing left for me but to die. For four hours she could get nothing else out of me, and I went away leaving her, I suspect, very vexed with a suitor who would dispute about a synonym.

I spent three or four months in this fashion becoming every day more amorous, for the reason that every day I ran upon a new obstacle that I had myself created. I was drawn to Mrs. Trevor's house, moreover, at least as much by my taste for gaming as by my ridiculous passion. Mrs. Trevor lent herself to my absurd manoeuvre with admirable patience. She answered all my letters, received me *tête-à-tête* and often kept me with her until three o'clock in the morning. But she gained nothing by this, nor did I. I was excessively timid, and frantically excited. I still had not learnt that one must take instead of asking. I always asked and never took. Mrs. Trevor must have found me a singular sort of suitor. Since, however, women always like whatever proves that they can inspire a grand passion, she accommodated herself to my behaviour, and received me none the worse.

I became jealous of an Englishman who took not the least interest in Mrs. Trevor, and sought to compel him to fight me. With the object of appeasing me, he stated that, far from wishing to take the wind out of my sails, he did not even find Mrs. Trevor attractive. I then wanted to fight him for failure to appreciate the woman I loved. Our pistols were already loaded when my Englishman, who had no desire for so ridiculous a duel, got out of it very cleverly. He demanded seconds, and informed me that he would tell them why I had picked a quarrel with him. In vain I urged that it was his duty to keep such a matter secret. He laughed at me, and I had to renounce my brilliant enterprise, in order not to compromise the lady of my aspirations.

At the beginning of the winter my father bade me make ready to follow him to Paris. My despair was boundless, and Mrs. Trevor appeared to be touched by it. I often took her in my arms and bedewed her hands with my tears. I would pass nights weeping on a bench where I had once seen her sitting. She wept with me, and had I been willing to cease disputing about words, perhaps I woud have had more complete successes. But the most that I achieved was a chaste kiss upon lips that were a suspicion faded. At length I departed, in a state of inexpressible grief. Mrs. Trevor promised to write to me, and I was led away.

My suffering was so visible that as long as two days afterwards one of my cousins, who was travelling with us, proposed to my father that he should send me back to Switzerland, since my cousin was persuaded that I could not support the journey. I supported it, however, and we arrived. I found a letter from Mrs. Trevor. It was couched in chilly terms, but I was grateful to her for keeping her promise. I replied in the most passionate language of love. I received a second letter, which was a little more meaningless than the first. I, on my side, became colder as our letters journeyed through the post. I wrote no more, and our liaison ended.

I saw Mrs. Trevor again, however, three months later, at Paris. I felt no emotion, and I think that what emotion she felt was caused only by surprise at seeing me so completely detached. The poor woman continued for a few years to ply her trade of coquet, incurring much ridicule, and then returned to England, where she became, so I have been told, nearly mad of a nervous complaint.

The first months of my stay at Paris were most agreeable. I again lived with M. Suard, and was received with perfect acceptance by his set. My wit, which at that time entirely lacked solidity and accuracy, had an amusingly epigrammatic turn; my learning, which was very desultory but superior to that of most of the men of letters of the rising generation, and the originality of my character—all these seemed novel and interesting. I was lionized by all the women of Madame Suard's set, whilst the men excused on grounds of age an impertinence that was the less noticeable and the less offensive because it was one, not of manners, but of opinions. Nevertheless, when I remember the sort of things I used to say at that time, and the convinced disdain that I showed towards everybody, I am still at a loss to know how I could have been tolerated. I remember that one day meeting a man of our set who was thirty years older than I was, I began talking with him. My conversation turned, as usual, on the absurdity of all the people whom we daily met. After thoroughly making fun of each of them, one after another, I suddenly shook the hand of the man with whom I was talking, and said: 'I have made you very merry at the expense of all our friends; but do not go on to suppose that, because I have made fun of them with you, I am obliged not to make fun of you with them. I warn you that there is no such understanding between us.'

Gaming, which had already got me into so much trouble, and has got me into so much trouble since, now again began to disturb my life and to spoil all that my father's kindness had done for me.

In Switzerland, at Mrs. Trevor's house, I had made the acquaintance of an elderly French lady, Madame de Bourbonne, who played to excess but was in other respects a kindly and rather original person. She played in her carriage, in bed, in her bath, morning, night, evening, always and everywhere, at every opportunity. I visited her in Paris, where she daily received a *quinze,* which she urged me to join. I regularly lost all the money that I brought there, and what I brought was the whole of my allowance from my father, and all I could borrow; which latter was, fortunately, not a great sum, although I neglected no means of running into debt.

I had in this connection a somewhat curious adventure with one of the oldest women of Madame Suard's set. She was Madame Saurin, wife of Saurin the philosopher and author of *Spartacus*. She had been very beautiful, and was the only person who remembered it, since she was sixty-five years old. She had shown me much friendship, and, although I was foolish enough to mock at her a little, I had more confidence in her than in any other person in Paris. One day I lost at Madame de Bourbonne's house all the money that I had, and all that I could lose on credit. Not knowing how to pay, it occurred to me to have recourse to Madame Saurin for a loan of the sum that I lacked. Since I myself, however, disapproved of this manœuvre, I wrote to her instead of speaking to her of the matter. I told her that I would come for her answer after dinner. This I did, and found her alone. My natural shyness, enhanced by the circumstances, caused me to wait a long time for her to be the first to mention my letter. At length, when she had said nothing about it, I resolved to break the silence. Blushing, with lowered eyes and in a voice of great emotion, I began to speak. 'You will perhaps be astonished,' I said, 'at my having approached you thus. I would be most unhappy to have given you an ill impression of myself by a thing that I would not have confided to you, had not your sweet kindness towards me encouraged me to do so. The confession which I have made to you, and which, as I fear from your silence, has wounded you, was extracted from me by an irresistible impulse of trust in you.'

I said all this with a pause after each word, not looking at Madame Saurin. Since she did not answer, however, I raised my eyes, and saw by her air of surprise that my harangue had utterly perplexed her.

I asked her if she had received my letter, and found

that she had not. This was still more of a facer, and I would willingly have had all my words unsaid, provided only that I could find some other means of escaping from my financial embarrassment. But I had no choice: I had to go on. I therefore resumed: 'You have been so kind to me, you have taken so much interest in me—perhaps I have presumed too much upon it. But there are moments when a man loses his head. I should never console myself if I had impaired your friendship. Allow me to speak to you no more of this unhappy letter. Let me conceal from you what escaped from me only in a moment of distress.'

'No,' she said to me. 'Why do you doubt my feelings? I wish to know all; go on, go on.' And she covered her face with her hands and trembled throughout her body. I clearly saw that she had taken all I had said to her as a declaration of love. This misunderstanding, her emotion and a great bed of red damask that was within two paces of us—these things filled me with an inexpressible terror. However, with the furious courage of a coward in revolt, I hastened to dispel her mistake. 'In truth,' I said to her, 'I know not why I should continue to annoy you so long with a matter of very little importance. I have been so foolish as to gamble, I have lost more than I at the moment possess, and I wrote to you to know if you could do me the service of lending me what I lack to pay my debt.'

Madame Saurin was for a moment motionless. Then her hands descended from her face, which it was no longer necessary to cover. She arose without saying a word, and counted out the money for which I had asked her. We were so confounded, she and I, that not a word passed between us. I did not open my mouth even to thank her.

II

IT WAS AT THIS TIME (1787) that I made acquaintance with the first woman of superior intelligence whom I had hitherto known, and one of the most intelligent I have ever met. Her name was Madame de Charrière. She was Dutch, of one of the first families of that country, and in her youth she had made a great stir with her wit and the strangeness of her character. Past her thirtieth year, after many affairs of the heart, of which some were rather unhappy, she married, against the wish of her family, her brothers' tutor, an intelligent man, of refined and noble character, but as cold and phlegmatic as could be imagined. During the first years of their marriage, she greatly tormented him with her efforts to implant in him a vivacity equal to her own; and her chagrin at not succeeding, except at moments, in this purpose quickly destroyed the happiness that she had promised herself from this in some respects disproportionate union.

She then took a lively fancy to a man much younger than herself, of very mediocre intelligence but most handsome appearance. I never knew all the details of this affair; but what she told me, and what I have learnt from other sources, are enough to show that she was very agitated and very unhappy; that her husband's disapproval disturbed her inward being; and that, when at length the young man who had caused this disapproval forsook her for another woman, whom he married, she spent some time in most frightful despair.

This despair turned out well for her literary reputation, for it was the inspiration of the best of her works: namely, *Caliste,* which is part of a novel published under the title *Letters Written from Lausanne.*

When I made her acquaintance she was occupied with seeing this book through the press. I was enchanted by her wit, and we spent days and nights in conversation. She was very severe in her judgments upon all she met, and I was by nature much given to mockery: we therefore suited each other perfectly. But we soon found more intimate and essential grounds of sympathy. Madame de Charrière had so original and vigorous an outlook upon life, such scorn for prejudices, so great a power of thought, so vigorous and disdainful a superiority to the human commonplace, that to me as I was at the age of twenty, as eccentric and disdainful as herself, her conversation was a joy hitherto unknown. I gave myself over to it utterly. Her husband, who was an excellent man and felt affec-

tion and gratitude towards her, had brought her to
Paris only to distract her from the grief into which
she had been plunged by the desertion of the man she
had loved. She was twenty-seven years older than I was,
so that our relationship could cause her husband no
disquiet. He was delighted by it, and did all he could
to encourage it. I still remember with emotion the
days and nights that we spent together, drinking tea
and talking with inexhaustible ardour on every possible subject.

Nevertheless, this new passion did not occupy my
whole time. I still had enough, unfortunately, in which
to incur a deal of debt. A woman who used to write
from Paris to my father informed him of my behaviour,
but wrote to him also that I could make all well if I
succeeded in marrying a young person who belonged
to the set in which I habitually moved, and who was
said to have an income of ninety thousand francs. This
idea, very naturally, had a great attraction for my
father. He communicated it to me in a letter which
also contained a great number of very just reproaches,
and at the end of which he declared that he would not
allow me to prolong my stay at Paris unless I endeavoured to realize this advantageous project, and
unless I believed that I had some chance of success.

The person in question was sixteen years of age, and
very pretty. Her mother had received me, ever since
my arrival in Paris, with much friendship. I saw myself placed between the necessity of at least attempting
a thing that might result greatly to my advantage, and
that of leaving a city where I found much entertainment, to rejoin a father who had announced great disapproval of me. I did not hesitate to take the risk. In
accordance with custom, I began by writing to the
mother to ask her daughter's hand. She answered in a
very friendly fashion, but with a refusal, for which
she offered the explanation that her daughter was
already promised to another, whom she was to marry
within a few months. Nevertheless, I do not believe
that the mother herself regarded this refusal as irrevocable: for, on the one hand, I have since learnt that
she made inquiries in Switzerland concerning my for-

tune; and, on the other hand, she gave me every opportunity of speaking with her daughter *tête-à-tête*. I behaved, however, like a real fool. Instead of profiting by the benevolence of the mother, who even whilst refusing me had shown me good will, I sought to embark upon a romance with the danghter, and began it in the most absurd fashion. I made no attempt to win her favour, I said to her not a single word of endearment. But I wrote her an eloquent letter, as if to a person whose parents wished to marry her against her will to a man whom she did not love, and I proposed that we should elope. Her mother, to whom she doubtless showed this strange letter, had the indulgence towards me to allow her daughter to answer as if she had told the mother nothing of the matter.

Mademoiselle Pourras—such was her name—wrote to me that it was for her parents to decide her future, and that it was not proper for her to receive letters from a man. I would not take this for an answer, and handsomely renewed my proposals of elopement, deliverance and protection against the marriage that was being forced upon her. One might have thought that I was writing to a victim who had implored my help, and to a person who had for me all the passion that I persuaded myself that I felt for her. The truth was that all my letters were addressed to a very reasonable little person, who loved me not at all, who had no repugnance against the man proposed for her, and had given me neither the occasion nor the right to address her in this fashion. But I had committed myself to this path, and not for the devil would I leave it.

What was even more inexplicable was that when I saw Mademoiselle Pourras I said not a word to her that had any connection with my letters. Her mother always left me alone with her, despite the extravagant proposals of which she surely knew: this strengthens my belief that I might yet have succeeded. But, far from profiting by these opportunities, I fell victim, each time I found myself alone with Mademoiselle Pourras, to an extreme shyness. I spoke to her only of insignificant matters, and did not even allude to the letters that I wrote her daily, nor to the sentiment that dictated them.

At length a circumstance with which I was not in the least involved caused a crisis that ended the whole affair. Madame Pourras, who all her life had carried her heart on her sleeve, still had a regular lover. Ever since I had asked her for her daughter's hand she had continued to show me friendship, and had always maintained the appearance of knowing nothing of my absurd correspondence. Thus, whilst I daily wrote to the daughter with proposals of elopement, I made the mother the confidante of my passion and sorrow. I did all this, I may say, spontaneously, and without the least bad faith; but such was the course to which I had committed myself with each of the two women.

It thus came about that Madame Pourras and I often had long conversations *tête-à-tête*. Her lover took umbrage. There were violent scenes, and Madame Pourras, who was nearly fifty and unwilling to lose a lover who might be her last, resolved to reassure him. I suspected nothing, and was one day making my usual lamentations to Madame Pourras, when in came M. de Sainte-Croix—this was the lover's name—and evinced much ill humour. Madame Pourras took me by the hand, led me up to him and asked whether I would solemnly declare to him that it was her daughter whom I loved and had asked in marriage, and that she herself was entirely unconnected with my assiduous visits to her home.

Madame Pourras had regarded the declaration that she demanded of me only as a means of putting an end to the resentment of M. de Sainte-Croix. I, however, viewed the matter in another light. I saw myself dragged before a stranger to confess to him that I was a disappointed lover, a man rejected by both mother and daughter. My wounded vanity threw me into a real fever. I happened to have in my pocket a small phial of opium, which I had for some time been carrying about with me. This was a result of my relationship with Madame de Charrière. She took a deal of opium to soothe her distress, thus giving me the idea of also obtaining some; and her conversation, always abundant and vigorous but very fantastic, kept me in a sort of mental drunkenness, which was in no small degree responsible for all the follies I committed at this period.

I had been in the habit of saying that I wished to kill myself, and had almost persuaded myself of this, although at bottom I had not the slightest desire to do so. Having my opium in a pocket, therefore, at the moment when, as I thought, I was being made a spectacle in the eyes of M. de Sainte-Croix, I felt an embarrassment from which it seemed easier to extract myself by a scene than by a quiet conversation. I foresaw that M. de Sainte-Croix would ask me questions and evince an interest in me. Since I considered myself humiliated, I could not endure the prospect of these questions or this interest, or of anything that might prolong the situation. I was confident that by swallowing my opium I would create a diversion from all this. Moreover, I had long entertained the notion that to seek to kill oneself for a woman is a method of pleasing her.

This notion is not exactly correct. When one already pleases a woman, and she only asks to give herself, it is good to threaten her with suicide, because one thus furnishes her with a decisive, rapid and honourable pretext. But when one is not loved, neither the threat nor the act has any effect. Throughout my whole adventure with Mademoiselle Pourras, my fundamental error was that I acted the drama entirely by myself.

Accordingly, when Madame Pourras had finished speaking, I replied that I thanked her for having put me in a situation which left only one course of action open to me. I then brought out my little phial and carried it to my lips. I remember that, in the brief instant that elapsed whilst I performed this operation, I presented myself with an alternative that finally decided me. 'If I die,' I said to myself, 'all will be over; and if I am saved, Mademoiselle Pourras will be bound to feel tenderly towards a man who has sought to kill himself for her.'

So I swallowed my opium. I do not think that there was enough of it to do me great harm; and since M.

de Sainte-Croix precipitated himself upon me, I spilt
more than half of it. There was great consternation,
and I was made to take acids to destroy the opium's
effect. I did what was asked of me with perfect docility,
not because I was afraid, but because they would have
insisted, and I should have found it too tedious to
argue. When I say that I was not afraid, I do not mean
that I knew how small the danger was. I was not at all
acquainted with the effects of opium, and believed them
much more terrible than they are. But after considering my alternative I was quite indifferent to what
might happen. Nevertheless, my complaisance in allowing myself to be given anything that might prevent
the effect of my action must have persuaded the spec-
tators that there was nothing serious about the whole
tragedy.

This was not the only time in my life that after a
dramatic action I have been suddenly unable to support the tedious solemnity necessary to keep it up, and
have out of sheer boredom undone my own work.
They administered to me all the remedies that they
thought proper, and preached me a little sermon, half
compassionate and half magisterial, to which I listened
with a tragic air. Mademoiselle Pourras, who had not
been present whilst I was playing the fool for her, now
entered the room, and I illogically had the delicacy to
aid the mother in her efforts to prevent the daughter
from noticing anything. The latter was dressed to go
to the Opera, where there was a first performance of
Tarare by Beaumarchais. Madame proposed that I
should accompany them, and I accepted. In order that
everything about this affair should be tragi-comic, my
attempt upon my life ended in an evening at the Opera.
I was actually in a state of wild gaiety, whether because the opium had produced this effect upon me, or
because—which seems to me more probable—I was disgusted with all the previous lugubrious events, and
felt a need of entertainment.

Madame Pourras saw the necessity of putting a term
to my extravagances, and on the following day she took
as her pretext my letters to her daughter, of which she
pretended to have that day learnt for the first time. She

wrote to me that I had abused her trust by proposing an elopement to her daughter whilst being received in her house. She declared that she would therefore no longer receive me; and to deprive me of any hope and any means of continuing my attempts she sent for M. de Charrière and begged him to question her daughter concerning her sentiments towards me. Mademoiselle Pourras very explicitly replied to M. de Charrière that I had never spoken to her of love; that she had been much astonished at my letters; that she had never said or done anything that could authorize me to make such proposals; that she loved me not at all; that she was highly content with the marriage that her parents had planned for her; and that she most freely associated herself with her mother's attitude towards me. M. de Charrière gave me an account of this conversation, adding that, if he had perceived in the young person the least inclination for me, he would have tried to influence the mother in my favour.

Thus the adventure ended. I cannot say that it caused me any great distress. The excitement of it had on occasions gone to my head; the fascination of an obstacle to be surmounted had inspired me with a sort of furious obstinacy; the fear of being obliged to return to my father had made me persevere in a desperate enterprise; and my stupidity had made me choose the most absurd methods, which my shyness had rendered still more absurd. But I do not think that at the bottom of my heart there had ever been any love. What is certain is that, within a day of my having to abandon my designs, I was completely consoled.

The person who, even whilst I was indulging in all these mad escapades, truly occupied my mind and heart was Madame de Charrière. In the midst of all the excitement of my romantic letters, my proposals of elopement, my threats of suicide and my theatrical taking of poison, I passed hours and whole nights talking with Madame de Charrière, and during these conversations forgot my troubles concerning my father, my debts, Mademoiselle Pourras and the entire world. I am convinced that, but for these conversations, my conduct would have been much less foolish. All Madame de Charrière's opinions were founded on disdain of all conventions and customs. We intoxicated one another with our jests and our scorn of the human race, and the result of it all was that I behaved as I spoke, sometimes laughing like a madman half an hour after some despairing act that I had committed in complete sincerity. The final result of all my designs upon Mademoiselle Pourras was that I became still more closely united with Madame de Charrière: she was the only person with whom I could speak freely, because she was the only one who did not plague me with advice and reproaches concerning my conduct.

Of the other women of the set in which I moved, some took a friendly interest in me, and preached to me at every opportunity; the others would, I think, not have been averse to taking in hand the education of a young man who seemed so passionate—as they gave me clearly enough to understand. Madame Suard had conceived a plan that I should marry. She sought to arrange a match for me with a girl of sixteen, who was fairly intelligent, highly affected, not at all pretty, and would be rich after the death of an elderly uncle.

(I may mention, between parentheses, that as I now write, in 1811, the uncle still lives. The young person in the meanwhile married M. Pastoret, who in the Revolution became famous for his doltishness. She had a few adventures; sought a divorce in order to marry a man whom I at one time knew well, and by whom she had a child; perpetrated several follies to achieve this end; and thereafter, having failed to do so, skilfully took refuge in prudery, and is today one of the best-thought-of women in Paris.)

At the time when Madame Suard singled me out for her, the girl was extremely desirous to have a husband, and used to tell everybody so with great frankness. But neither the designs of Madame Suard, nor the advances of certain elderly ladies, nor the sermons of certain others had any effect on me. For a partner in marriage I wanted only Mademoiselle Pourras.

In point of looks, Mademoiselle Pourras was still my preference. In point of intelligence, I saw, heard and cherished only Madame de Charrière. This does not mean, however, that I failed to profit by the few hours during which we were separated, to indulge in still further follies.

I no longer remember who brought me to the house of a damsel styling herself the Comtesse de Linières. She came from Lausanne, where her father was a butcher. A young Englishman had abducted her, by setting fire to the house in which she lived. After being forsaken by this first lover she had continued to ply a trade that her pretty looks rendered lucrative. When she had amassed some money, she made a match with a certain M. de Linières, who died soon after. Having thus become a widow and a comtesse, she kept a gaming-house. She was at least forty-five, but, so as not entirely to renounce her former standing in the community, she had brought to stay with her a young sister, about twenty years of age, tall, fresh, shapely and of a delightful stupidity. Amongst the men who visited her house were a few gentlemen, and not a few scoundrels. I was eagerly received there, for lack of anyone better. I would pass half my nights in losing my money; would then go to talk with Madame de Charrière, who never went to bed until six o'clock in the morning; and would sleep half the day.

I do not know whether a report of this fine way of life came to the ears of my father, or whether it was merely the news of my lack of success with Mademoiselle Pourras that decided him to remove me from Paris. At any rate, just when I expected it least, I was visited by a M. Benay, a lieutenant in my father's regiment, who had instructions to bring me to him at Bois-le-Duc.

I felt that I deserved much reproach; and the confusion of ideas into which I had been plunged by my conversations with Madame de Charrière caused me to shrink from the prospect of what I believed myself destined to hear. I resigned myself to it, nevertheless, and the idea of disobeying my father did not at first occur to me.

Our departure was delayed, however, by a difficulty in obtaining a carriage. My father had left with me in

Paris the old carriage in which we had arrived there; but in my financial embarrassment I had thought fit to sell it. M. Benay, relying upon this carriage, had come in a little cabriolet with room for only one. We tried to obtain a post-chaise from the livery-stable-keeper to whom I had sold my father's; but he had none, or would not lend us one. This difficulty held us up for a day, during which my head continued to be in a whirl, of which Madame de Charrière's conversation was in no small part the cause. She surely could not have foreseen the effect that it would produce upon me; but by ceaselessly entertaining me with the stupidity of the human species and the absurdity of prejudices, and by sharing my admiration for all that was fantastical, extraordinary and original, she ended by inspiring me with a veritable thirst to find myself, too, beyond the human pale. I made no particular plans, but borrowed from Madame de Charrière, purely by chance and with I know not what confused idea in my head, the sum of thirty louis.

On the following day M. Benay came to discuss with me how we should travel, and we agreed that we should follow one another in one-passenger vehicles, making the best arrangements we could. As he had never seen Paris, I proposed that we should not depart until the evening, to which he readily agreed. I had no clear motive for this proposal, but it delayed by so much a moment that I dreaded. I had my thirty louis in my pocket, and felt a sort of pleasure in telling myself that I was still master of my actions.

We went to dine at the Palais-Royal, where chance placed at my side a man whom I had sometimes met at the house of Madame de Bourbonne, and with whom I had enjoyed conversing since he was a person of some wit. I still remember his name, which has been graven in my memory by the circumstances in which we met for the last time—it was on the 24th of June, 1787. His name was the Chevalier de La Roche Saint-André, a fine chemist and a man of talent, a player for great stakes and a man much sought after. I accosted him, and, full as I was of my own situation, took him aside and poured out my heart. He listened to me probably with but one ear, as I would have done in his place.

During my harangue I mentioned to him that I sometimes wished to put an end to my troubles by running away. 'Where to?' he remarked, quite casually.

'Why, to England,' I answered.

'Yes, indeed,' he said, 'it is a fine country, and one is quite free there.'

'When I returned,' I said, 'everything would be settled.'

'Certainly,' he replied, 'everything settles itself, in time.'

M. Benay came up to us, and I returned with him to finish our dinner. But my conversation with M. de La Roche Saint-André had a twofold effect upon me: first, by showing to me that others would attach very little importance to an escapade that had hitherto seemed to me a most terrible thing; and secondly, by putting into my head the notion of England—a notion which set a direction for my course, in case I should run away. This certainly did not mean that I had the least motive for going to England, any more than before, or that I could expect the least help there; but my imagination was, at least, directed towards one country rather than another. Meanwhile I felt at first no more than a sort of impatience at the thought that the period in which I could take my own decisions was about to elapse, or rather had elapsed already; for we were to take the road immediately after dinner, and probably M. Benay would not leave me in the meanwhile.

As we left table, I met the Chevalier de La Roche, who said to me jestingly: 'What, so you are not gone yet?' These words increased my regret at being no longer free to do what they indicated. We went to our rooms, we packed our trunks, the carriage came and we climbed aboard. I sighed to think that on this occasion everything had been decided, and gloomily clutched at the useless thirty louis in my pocket. We were horribly crowded in the little one-passenger cabriolet. I was at the back, and M. Benay, who was rather tall and very bulky, was seated on a little chair between my legs, shaken up and down, and at each jolt losing his balance and knocking his head to the right or left. Before we had gone a few yards he began to complain. I outdid him in complaints, since it occurred to me that, if we turned back, I should again be at liberty to do what I wanted. As it happened, before we had reached the city limits he declared that he could endure the journey no longer and asked me to postpone it until the following day, and in the meanwhile find another mode of travel. I consented, and took him back to his hotel. So there I was, back home at eleven o'clock in the evening, with ten or twelve hours in which to deliberate.

It did not take me all this time to decide on an act of folly far graver and more blameworthy than any that I had hitherto committed. I did not, however, see it in this light. My head had been turned both by fear of seeing my father again and by all the sophistry that I had repeated and heard others repeat on the subject of independence. I paced up and down my room for half an hour. Then, taking a spare shirt and my thirty louis, I went down the stairs and asked to be shown the door-rope. The door opened, and I rushed into the street.

I still did not know what I wished to do. In general, the thing that throughout my life has most helped me to adopt courses of action which, although highly absurd, have at least seemed to entail great decision of character, has been precisely the complete absence of such decision, and the feeling I have always had that what I was doing was not at all irrevocable. The upshot has always been that, reassured by my very uncertainty concerning the consequences of an act of folly which I have kept telling myself I would perhaps not commit, I have taken one step after another until the folly was an accomplished fact.

It was exactly in this fashion that I now let myself be drawn into my ridiculous flight. I meditated for a few moments on what refuge I should choose for the night, and went to ask hospitality of a person of easy virtue, whom I had known at the beginning of the winter. She received me with professional tenderness, but I told her that my visit was unconnected with her charms; that I had to make a journey of several days, to a distance of fifty leagues from Paris; and that she must find me a hired post-chaise for the morrow, at as early an hour as she could arrange. Meanwhile, since I was in great distress of mind, I wished to collect my energies, and asked for Champagne wine; a few glasses of which deprived me of what little faculty of reflection I had left. I then fell into a somewhat disturbed sleep. When I awoke, I found a livery-stable-keeper in attendance. He let me out a chaise at so-much a day, without inquiring after my route, and merely obtaining a receipt from me, which I signed with a fictitious name, having the fixed intention of sending the vehicle back to him from Calais. My damsel had also ordered post-horses for me. I paid her suitably, and found myself at full gallop for England, with twenty-seven louis in my pocket, and not having had time to return to my senses for a single instant.

In twenty-two hours I was at Calais. I entrusted M. Dessin with the task of sending my chaise back to Paris, and inquired after a packet. One was sailing within the hour. I had no passport, but in those happy days there were none of the difficulties that have encumbered every movement since the French, in seeking to be free, have imposed slavery upon themselves and upon others. An attendant hired for the occasion undertook for six francs to take care of the necessary formalities, and within three quarters of an hour after my arrival at Calais I was on board.

I arrived that evening at Dover, found a travelling-companion who wished to go to London, and on the morning of the following day I was in this immense city: without a being whom I knew, without any kind of purpose, and with fifteen louis as my entire fortune. I first of all sought lodging at a house in which I had lived for a few days on my last passage through London. I felt a need to see a familiar face. There was no room for me, but the landlord found me one close by. Once lodged, my first care was to write to my father. I asked his forgiveness for my strange escapade, making what excuses I could. I told him that I had suffered horribly in Paris, and that, above all, I was weary of human beings. I penned some philosophic phrases on the fatiguing nature of society and the need for solitude. I asked his leave to spend three months in England in absolute retirement, and concluded, with a truly comic inconsequence, which I myself did not notice, by telling him of my wish to marry and to live, with my wife, peacefully at his side.

The truth was that I scarcely knew what to write; that I had indeed a real need for six months' repose from moral and physical excitement; and that, finding myself for the first time completely alone and completely free, I burned to enjoy this unknown state of solitude, to which I had for so long aspired. I had no uneasiness about money; for I immediately spent two of my fifteen louis on two dogs and a monkey. I brought these fine purchases back to my lodging. But I quickly quarrelled with the monkey. I tried to strike him for his correction; but he became so angry that, little though he was, I could not keep the upper hand. I took him back to the animal-shop where I had obtained him, and was given in exchange a third dog. But I soon grew weary of this menagerie, and sold back two of my beasts for a quarter of what they had cost me. My third dog attached itself to me with true devotion, and was my faithful companion during the preregrinations upon which I soon afterwards embarked.

My life in London, if I leave out of account the uneasiness caused me by ignorance of my father's attitude, was neither expensive nor disagreeable. I paid a half-guinea a week for my lodging, spent about three shillings a day on my food, and about another three on incidental expenses; so that my thirteen louis seemed capable of providing me with subsistence for nearly a month. But after two days I conceived the project of making a tour of England, and set about making provision for it. I remembered the address of my father's banker, who advanced me twenty-five louis. I also discovered the dwelling of a young man whom I had known at Lausanne, in Madame Trevor's circle, and to whom I had shown many civilities. I went to see him. He was a handsome youth, more infatuated with his own appearance than anyone else I have known. He used to spend three hours having his hair dressed, holding a mirror so that he might himself supervise the arrangement of each lock. He was not without intelligence, however, and was fairly well read in ancient literature, like almost all young Englishmen of the upper class. His fortune was very considerable, and he was of distinguished family. His name was Edward Lascelles, and he was at one time a Member of Parliament, but a somewhat obscure one.

I went, then, to visit this young man. He received me politely, but appeared not to have retained the least memory of our previous connection. Nevertheless, since in the course of our conversation he made several inquiries as to how he could be of service to me, and since I was continually thinking of my journey to the English provinces, I suggested that he should lend me fifty louis. He refused, excusing himself more or less adroitly by the absence of his banker, and I know not what other pretexts. His valet, a worthy Swiss who knew my family, wrote to offer me forty guineas; but his letter was delivered to my address whilst I was out of London, and reached me only a long time afterwards, when he had already made some other use of his money.

It happened that in the house next to mine was lodging one of my old Edinburgh friends, John Mackay by name, who held some rather subordinate post in London. We were delighted to see each other; I especially so, at no longer being in such absolute solitude. I spent several hours a day with him, although he was a man of far from distinguished intellect; but he brought back to me agreeable memories, and I liked him, amongst other reasons, because of our common friendship for a man whom I mentioned in my account of my life at Edinburgh; that John Wilde who was so notable for his gifts and character, and who came to such an unhappy end. John Mackay afforded me yet another pleasure of the same sort by giving me the address of one of our comrades whom I had known at the same period. This procured me several agreeable evenings, but in no way furthered my plans. The result was, however, that I had a new motive for putting them into execution, since these encounters so vividly reminded me of my stay in Scotland. I wrote to John Wilde, and received an answer so full of friendship that I resolved not to leave England without having seen him.

Meanwhile I continued to live in London, dining frugally, sometimes going to spectacles or even frequenting the society of wenches; spending my journey-money, doing nothing, sometimes bored, at other times uneasy about my father and seriously reproaching myself; but finding, nevertheless, an indescribable sense of happiness in my untrammelled freedom.

One day, whilst turning a street corner, I found myself face to face with another Edinburgh student, who had become a doctor of medicine and had found a fairly advantageous situation in London. His name was Richard Kentish, and he has since made a reputation with some moderately well-thought-of works. Our connection at Edinburgh had not been very close, but we had sometimes found entertainment in each other's company. He evinced great delight at meeting me again, and immediately took me to see his wife, whom I knew from of old. When I was nearing the end of my studies, he had taken her to Gretna Green to marry her—as is the custom when relatives refuse their consent to a marriage—and had afterwards brought her to Edinburgh to present her to his old acquaintances.

She was a small woman, thin, dry, not pretty, and, I think, rather domineering. She received me most civilly. They were leaving next day for Brighthelmstone, and urged me to go with them, promising me all sorts of pleasures there. This was exactly the opposite route to that which I wished to take; so I declined. But two days later it occurred to me that I might as well amuse myself there as elsewhere, and I took a seat on a diligence which brought me there in a day, together with a turtle destined to be eaten by the Prince of Wales. On my arrival I established myself in a poor little room, and at once went in search of Kentish, having taken his word for it that I should lead the gayest life imaginable. But he did not know a cat, was not received in good society, and spent his time in looking after some sick people for money, and in observing others for his instruction. All this was very useful to him, but did not correspond to my hopes.

However, I spent eight or ten days at Brighthelmstone, because I had no reason to expect better things anywhere else, and because this first experience discouraged me—although wrongly, as will be seen—with my Edinburgh project. At length, having become daily more bored, one afternoon I suddenly departed. What decided me to do so was an encounter with a man who offered to share with me the cost of the journey to London. I left a note of farewell for Kentish, and we arrived in London at midnight. I had been much afraid that we might be robbed, for I had all my money on me and would not have known where to turn. I therefore held all the time between my legs a small sword-stick, with the firm resolve to defend myself and be killed rather than yield up my treasure. My travelling-companion— who probably did not have his whole fortune on him, as I had—laughed at my resolve. The journey passed off, however, without my having any opportunity to display my courage.

Back in London, I let several more days pass in idleness. To my great surprise, my independence began to weigh heavily on me. Tired of scouring the streets of this city where there was nothing to interest me, and seeing my resources dwindle, I at length took post-horses and went to Newmarket. I know not what decided me in favour of this spot, unless it was that the name recalled to me the horse-races, betting and gambling of which I had heard so much. But it was not the season; there was not a soul in the place. I spent two days there, wondering what to do next.

I wrote very affectionately to my father, assuring him that I would return to him without delay. I counted my money, which I found reduced to sixteen guineas. Then, after paying my host, I slipped away on foot, following my nose, with the resolve to make for Northampton, near which lived a certain Mr. Bridges whom I had known at Oxford. On the first day I made twenty-eight miles in torrential rain. Nightfall caught me on the deserted and gloomy moors of the county of Norfolk, and I again began to fear that robbers might come and put an end to all my adventures and pilgrimages by stripping me of all my resources. I arrived, however, safe and sound at a litle village called Stokes. I was most unfittingly received at the inn, because I had been seen to arrive on foot, and in England only beggars and those thieves of the worst type, who are known as 'foot-pads,' travel in this manner. I was given a bad bed, for which I had difficulty in obtaining sheets. I slept very well, however, and next morning, by dint of complaining and giving myself airs, I succeeded in exacting the treatment due to a gentleman—and in having to pay a reckoning in proportion.

I did this purely for dignity's sake, since after breakfast I set out on foot, and went fourteen miles to dine at Lynn, a little market town, where I again halted, because I was beginning to dislike this manner of travel. I began by swallowing a great bowl of negus, which the inn had ready. I then tried to make some arrangements for the continuance of my journey; but suddenly I found myself completely drunk, to the point of feeling that I no longer knew what I was doing and could in no way answer for myself. I had enough good sense, however, to be highly frightened at being in such a state in a strange town, all alone and with so little money in my pocket. It was a very singular sensation, to be thus at the mercy of the first comer, and to lack all means of answering, of defending myself, or of controlling my movements. I locked my door, and, thus protected from my fellow-men, laid myself on the ground to wait until my wits should return.

I spent five or six hours in this position, the fantastical nature of which, together with the effects of the wine, made upon me such strange and vivid impressions that I have always remembered them. There I was, three hundred leagues from home, without property or any means of subsistence, not knowing whether my father had disowned and rejected me for ever, with enough to live on for a fortnight—and having brought myself into this situation without any need or purpose. My reflections in this drunken state were much more serious and more reasonable than those that came to me when I had enjoyed the full use of my faculties; because then I had made plans, and been conscious of my power to act; whereas now the wine had deprived me of this power, and my brains were in too much of a whirl for me to be capable of occupying myself with any plan. Gradually my wits returned, and I was sufficiently restored in the use of my faculties to inquire after means of continuing my journey in greater comfort. The replies were not satisfactory. I had not enough money to buy an old horse for which I was asked twelve louis. I again took a post-chaise, thus adopting the most expensive method of travel precisely because I had almost nothing, and spent the night at a little town called Wisbeach.

On the road I met a handsome equipage that had overturned. In it were a lady and gentleman, to whom I offered places in my chaise. They accepted, and I was pleased to think that this encounter would result in my spending a less solitary evening. But, to my great surprise, the lady and gentleman curtsied and bowed and left me without saying a word.

Next day I learnt that an inferior company of strolling players was performing in a neighbouring barn. Thinking that I was as well in that place as in any other, I decided to remain there and see the spectacle. I do not remember what the piece was!

At length, on the following day, I took another post-chaise and went to Thrapston, the nearest town to the parish of Wadenho, where I counted on finding Mr. Bridges. I took a horse at the inn, and at once proceeded to Wadenho.

Mr. Bridges was, indeed, as I had thought, the parish priest of this village; but he was away from home, and was not due to return for three weeks. This news upset all my plans. I had no more means of obtaining the necessary money to go to Scotland; no acquaintance in the neighbourhood; scarcely enough with which to return to London and live there for a fortnight—and that was not even enough time in which to expect an answer from my father. I could not deliberate for long, for each dinner and each bed put me in a more embarrassing situation. I took my departure.

I realized, after strict calculation, that I could reach

Edinburgh, travelling on horseback or by coach. Once there, I counted on my friends: a charming result of youth; for certainly if today I had to cover a hundred leagues in order to throw myself on the mercy of people who were under no obligation to me, whilst I myself was under no necessity that might excuse such a proceeding; if I had to expose myself to questions concerning my past behaviour and refusals of my requests for what I might need or desire—nothing on earth could bring me to do this. But in my twentieth year nothing seemed simpler than to say to my college friends: 'I have come three hundred leagues to sup with you. I haven't a halfpenny, invite me, cherish me, let us drink together, thank me for coming and lend me money for my return.' I was convinced that such a mode of address would delight them.

I accordingly sent for my host and told him that I wished to use my friend Bridges' absence as an opportunity for going on a visit of a few days to a place a few miles distant, and that he was to procure a carriage for me. He brought me a man who had one, and also a very good horse. Unfortunately the carriage was at Stamford, a little town ten miles away. He made no difficulty about letting it out to me, and lent me his horse, and his son as a guide, to take me to the livery-stable that had been repairing the carriage. It was agreed that I should take the carriage on from Stamford. I was very pleased that the affair had been so easily settled, and I mounted the horse next day. The son of the man to whom it belonged appeared on a feeble little nag lent him by the host at the inn, and we arrived quite safely at Stamford.

Here, however, a great misfortune awaited me. The carriage was not yet repaired, and I looked in vain for another. I proposed to my young guide that he should allow me to continue my journey on his father's horse. He refused. He might perhaps have been persuaded, but at his first refusal I flew into a furious rage and hurled abuse at him. He laughed at me. I then tried to win him by blandishments, but he said that I had treated him too ill, mounted his horse and left me. My embarrassment grew every minute. I went to bed at Stamford in real despair.

Next day I determined to return to Thrapston in the hope of getting my host to find me another vehicle. When I reopened the question with him, I found him very little disposed to consent. A rather strange circumstance, at which I would never have guessed, had given him a very bad opinion of me. Since getting drunk at Lynn, I had had a sort of repugnance to wine, and a fear of the state in which I had for some hours been sunk. Consequently, during all my stay at the inn at Thrapston, I had drunk only water. This abstemiousness, not at all usual in England, had seemed to my host a real scandal. It was not he who told me of the ill impression he had received of me, but the man who had previously let me out a carriage, and for whom I again sent to try to renew the same arrangements with him. When I complained to him of his son's behaviour, he replied: 'Ah, sir, they say such strange things about you!'

This much surprised me, and I pressed him for an explanation. 'You have not drunk a drop of wine since you came here,' he answered.

I got off my high horse, and sent for a bottle of wine immediately; but the mischief was done, and I could get nothing. I had to make my decision immediately. I again hired a horse for the morrow, on the pretext of going to Wadenho to see whether Mr. Bridges had arrived. Mischance would have it that of my host's two horses only the worst was in the stable. So all I had for a mount was a tiny white gelding, very old and horribly ugly.

I left early next morning, and from a distance of twelve miles wrote to my host that I had met a friend who was going to see the horse-races at Nottingham, and that I had undertaken to accompany him. I did not know the risk that I was running. English law regards the use of a hired horse for a destination other than that first stated, as theft. It therefore depended on the horse's owner whether or not he would have me prosecuted, or a notice for my arrest put in the newspapers. I would have been most certainly arrested and brought to justice, and perhaps condemned to deportation to the Isles; or I would, at the very least, have been proceeded against for theft; which, even supposing I had been acquitted, would have been highly disagreeable and, in view of my whole escapade, would have produced a terrible effect wherever it became known. In the event, nothing of the sort occurred. The owner of the horse was at first a little astonished. But he went to Wadenho, where by a happy chance he found Mr. Bridges arrived back. The latter, who had received a message from me, answered for my return.

For my part, suspecting nothing of all this I rode the first day some twenty miles, and slept at Kettering, which is a little village in Leicestershire if I remember rightly. Now, truly and for the first time, I experienced that bliss of independence and solitude to which I had so often looked forward. In my previous wanderings I had had no fixed plan, and had been discontented with a vagabondage that I rightly regarded as absurd and purposeless. Now I had a purpose: one of very little importance, I will grant, since my only object was to pay a fortnight's visit to some college friends. All the same, I was proceeding in a fixed direction, and I took fresh life from knowing my own mind.

I have forgotten the various places where I halted with my ugly little white horse. All that I remember is that the whole route was delightful. The country through which I passed was a garden. I went by Leicester, Derby, Buxton, Shortley, Kendall, Carlisle. From there I entered Scotland, and arrived at Edinburgh. I took so much pleasure in the journey that I seek to recall the least circumstance of it. I covered from thirty to fifty miles a day. On the first two days I was a little shy at the inns. My mount was so puny that I felt that I seemed no richer or more 'gentleman-like' than when I had journeyed on foot; and I remembered the bad reception I had experienced when travelling in this fashion. But I soon learnt that public opinion drew an immense distinction between the traveller on foot and the traveller on horseback. The commercial houses in England have agents who journey all over the kingdom in the latter fashion, on visits to their correspondents. These commercial travellers live very well and spend much money at the inns, so that they are warmly welcomed. The prices of a dinner and of a bed are fixed, because the inn-keepers make their profits on the wine. I was everywhere regarded as one of these commercial travellers, and was therefore wonderfully well received. At every inn there were seven or eight of them, with whom I would converse: when they discovered that I was of a class superior to theirs, they treated me all the better. England is the country where, on the one hand, the rights of each person are the best protected and, on the other hand, differences in station are the most respected.

I travelled for almost nothing. The total expenses of myself and my horse did not amount to a half-guinea a day. The beauty of the countryside, the season and the roads, the cleanliness of the inns, the inhabitants' air of happiness, good sense and settled living are a source of perpetual rejoicing to any observant traveller. I knew the language well enough to be taken for an Englishman; or rather, for a Scot, since I had retained the Scotch accent from my earlier education in Scotland.

I at length arrived at Edinburgh on the 12th of August, at six o'clock in the evening, with about nine or ten shillings in my pocket. I made haste to seek out my friend Wilde, and within two hours of my arrival was in the midst of all those of my acquaintances who were still in the city: for at this time of year the wealthier of them were on their estates. Enough of them, however, remained for our gathering to be numerous, and they all received me with real transports of joy. They were delighted with the singularity of my expedition, a thing that always has an attraction for the English.

Our communal life during the fortnight spent at Edinburgh was a continual festivity. My friends regaled me, each to the best of his ability, and all our evenings and nights were spent together. Poor Wilde, especially, took a pleasure in entertaining me which he showed in the most simple and touching manner. Who would have then said that seven years later he would be chained to a pallet!

At length I had to think of returning. It was to Wilde that I applied for help. He obtained for me, with some difficulty but with the best grace in the world, the sum of ten guineas. I remounted my beast and set out.

Meanwhile I had gone to see, at Niddin, the Wauchopes who had given me so kindly a welcome when I was a student. I had learnt that the eldest sister was at a small town—a watering-place, if I am not mistaken—called Moffat. Although I could not too well afford a detour, I wished to visit her: I know not why, for she was not at all an agreeable person, being between thirty and thirty-five years of age, ugly, raw-boned, sour and capricious to the last degree. But I was in such good humour and so pleased with the welcome that I had received, that I did not wish to miss an opportunity of again seeing one of these good Scots people whom I was about to leave for an unlimited period. (I have, in fact, never seen any of them again.)

I found Miss Wauchope living by herself in her own establishment, as suited her character. She was touched by my visit, and proposed that on my journey to London I should accompany her through the counties of Cumberland and Westmorland. A man without means, who was a protégé of hers, joined our party, and we made a sufficiently agreeable trip. The profit I had of it was that I saw a part of England that I would not have seen otherwise; for I am so idle, and have so little curiosity, that I have never of my own accord gone to see a monument, nor a region, nor a famous man. I remain where chance throws me, until I take a leap that carries me to some quite other sphere. But I am not activated by a taste for amusement, nor by tedium—the two motives that usually decide men's modes of living. I must be seized by a dominant idea that takes possession of me and becomes a passion. This is why I appear a quite reasonable being to people who see me in the intervals between these engrossing passions, whilst I am making my terms with a most unattractive mode of life, and seeking no kind of distraction.

Westmorland, and Cumberland, too, in its beautiful part—for it has another part which is horrible—are like a small counterpart of Switzerland. They have some quite high mountains, whose summits are enveloped in mists instead of being covered with snow, lakes dotted with verdurous islands, fine trees, pretty little towns, and two or three clean and well-kept cities. Add to these the complete freedom to come and go without a living soul paying any attention, and with nothing to remind you of a police who make the guilty their pretext and the innocent their target. All these things make any trip in England a real joy.

At Keswick I saw, in a sort of museum, a copy of the sentence upon Charles I, with exact imitations of the signatures of all his judges: I gazed with curiosity at that of Cromwell, who until the commencement of this century could pass as a bold and able usurper but is nowadays regarded as unworthy of mention.

After accompanying me as far, I think, as Carlisle, Miss Wauchope left me, telling me, as her last counsel, to commit no more acts of folly similar to the escapade that had given her the pleasure of again seeing me. From there I journeyed on, with precisely enough money to bring me to the home of Mr. Bridges, where I hoped to obtain further means of subsistence. I felt more and more satisfied with this mode of life, in which, as I well remember, my only regret was that a moment might come when old age would prevent me from travelling thus, alone and on horseback. But I consoled myself with the promise that I would continue so to live as long as I could.

I arrived at length at Wadenho, where I found everything prepared for my reception. Mr. Bridges was not at home, but returned next day. He was an excellent man, almost fanatically devout, but utterly disposed in my favour, being persuaded—although I never told him so—that I had come from Paris expressly to see him. He kept me with him for several days, introduced me to my neighbours and set me financially afloat. Amongst the people to whom he presented me, I remember only Lady Charlotte Wentworth, aged about seventy, whom I gazed at with especial veneration because she was the sister of the Marquis of Rockingham, and my Scottish politics had filled me with enthusiasm for the Whig administration of which he had been the leader.

In response to all the kindnesses shown me by Mr. Bridges, I willingly accommodated myself to all his

religious observances, although they were considerably
different from mine. Every evening he assembled some
young people of whose education he had taken charge,
two or three servants of his household, farm-hands,
stable-men and others, read to them some passages from
the Bible, and then made us all kneel whilst he uttered
long and fervent prayers. Often he literally rolled on
the ground, striking his forehead on the wooden floor
and repeatedly beating his breast. The least distraction
during these exercises, which often continued for more
than an hour, would throw him into a real despair.

Nevertheless I would willingly have resigned myself
to staying with Mr. Bridges indefinitely, so great was
my fear becoming of presenting myself before my father.
But there was no possibility of further delay, so I fixed
the day of my departure. I had returned to its proprietor
the faithful little white horse that had carried me
throughout my journey. A passion for this manner of
travel gave me the notion of buying one, without thinking of the difficulty that I would have in leaving England. Mr. Bridges went bail for me, and I found myself
again on the road to London, much better mounted
than before, and highly pleased with my plan to return
to my father in this fashion.

I arrived in London some time in September, and all
my fine hopes were shattered. I had been well able to
explain to Mr. Bridges why I had no money when I
arrived at his house. But I had not confided to him that
I would be equally embarrassed in London. He believed,
on the contrary, that once I was there the bankers to
whom my father was supposed to have referred me
would furnish what funds I needed. He had, therefore,
lent me in ready cash the sum sufficient for my journey.

The most reasonable course would have been to sell
my horse, take a seat on a diligence and return to my
inevitable destination in the obscurest and cheapest
fashion possible. But I clung to my adopted mode of
travel, and set about finding other resources. Kentish
came to my mind; I went to see him, and he promised
to help me out of my difficulty. On the strength of this
promise, I had no other thought than to profit by the
little time remaining in which to enjoy an independence

that I should so soon lose. I spent in various ways what little I had left, and became penniless. Letters from my father, which reached me at the same time, awoke a remorse that was increased by my disagreeable situation. He expressed deep despair concerning my whole conduct and prolonged absence, and informed me that, to compel me to rejoin him, he had forbidden his bankers to give me any help at all.

I at length spoke of the matter to Kentish, who at once changed his tone. Instead of condoling with me on my position, he told me that I should not have put myself in it. I still remember the impression that this answer produced on me. For the first time I was at the mercy of a man who let me know it. Kentish did not wish exactly to abandon me, but, whilst still offering me his help, he did not conceal either his disapproval of my conduct or the fact that it was only pity that moved him to aid me; and his assistance took the most wounding forms. To dispense with the necessity of lending me a farthing, he proposed that I should come to dine with him daily; and, to make me feel that he looked upon me, not as an invited friend, but as a poor recipient of bounty, he for five or six days affected to have for dinner only what was required for his wife and himself—repeatedly saying that his household was arranged only for two people.

I endured this insolence, because I had written to the bankers, despite my father's prohibition, and hoped to find myself in a position to show my self-styled benefactor what I really thought of his behaviour. But these wretched bankers were, or pretended to be, out of the city, and kept me waiting a whole week for their answer. When it came, it was a formal refusal. I therefore had to have a final explanation with Kentish. He advised me to sell my horse and use the proceeds to go, as best I could, wherever I would. The only service that he offered me was to take me to a coper who would buy my horse immediately. I had no alternative; and after an affectionate scene, in which I would have had a thorough quarrel with him if he had not shown himself as insensible to my reproaches as he had been to my prayers, we went together to visit the man of whom he had spoken. The coper offered me four louis for a horse that had cost me fifteen. I was so enraged that, at his first words, I was extremely rude to this person—who, after all, was only following his trade—and was nearly knocked down by his men. This affair having come to nothing, Kentish, who was beginning to be as eager to be done with it as I was, offered to lend me ten guineas, on condition that I gave him a letter of exchange for this sum, and also left him with the horse, which he promised to sell as best he could on my behalf. I was not sufficiently master of the situation to refuse anything.

I therefore accepted Kentish's proposal, and departed, vowing never again to get myself into such a situation. My lingering taste for expeditions on horseback made me decide to ride to Dover at post-haste. This mode of travel is not customary in England, where one can journey as quickly and more cheaply by post-chaise. But I thought it beneath my dignity not to have a horse between my legs.

The poor dog who had faithfully accompanied me on all my wanderings fell a victim to this last act of folly. (When I say 'this last,' I mean the last I committed in England, which I left next day.) He collapsed from fatigue a few miles from Dover. I entrusted him, almost dying, to a postilion, with a letter to Kentish, in which I informed him that, as he treated his friends like dogs, I hoped that he would treat this dog like a friend.

I learnt several years afterwards that the postilion had carried out my commission, and that Kentish had shown the dog to one of my cousins, who was travelling in England, telling him that it was a pledge of the intimate and tender friendship by which he and I were eternally bound. In 1794 Kentish thought fit to write to me in the same strain, reminding me of the delightful days we had spent together in 1787. I answered somewhat drily, and have never heard of him since.

At the moment when I set foot in Dover, a packet was about to leave for Calais. I was received on board, and on the 1st of October I was back in France. That is the last time I saw England, refuge of all that is noble, abode of happiness, wisdom and liberty, but a country where one must not unreservedly rely on the promises of old college friends. Yet I am an ingrate—I found twenty good ones, to a single bad.

At Calais, there was a new embarrassment. I calculated that I had no means of arriving at Bois-le-Duc, where my father was, with what was left of my ten guineas. I sounded M. Dessin, but he was too well accustomed to similar proposals by all the adventurers going to or from England to be much inclined to listen to me. I at length applied to a domestic at the inn, who, on the security of a watch worth ten louis, lent me three louis, a sum that was still not sufficient to ensure my arrival. I then again took horse, to ride day and night to the place where all I had to expect was displeasure and reproaches.

As I passed through Bruges I fell into the hands of an old coaching-stage proprietor, who had enough perspicacity to know by my face that he could make a dupe of me. He began by telling me that he had no horses, and would have none for several days; but he offered to procure a pair for me, at an excessive price. This bargain driven, he told me that the horse-keeper had no carriage. I had either to drive a new bargain, or suffer loss on the old one. I chose the first course. But when I thought everything settled, there was no postilion, and I obtained one only on exorbitant terms. My heart was so devoured by gloomy reflections, concerning the despair in which I supposed my father to be plunged—his last letters had been harrowing—the reception I would encounter, and the state of dependence awaiting me, of which I had lost the habit, that I had not the strength to wax indignant or to dispute about anything. I therefore submitted myself to all the rascalities of the scoundrelly coaching-stage proprietor, and at last was again on the road.

But my journey was not to be a quick one. It was about ten o'clock when I left Bruges, overwhelmed with fatigue. I fell asleep almost at once. After a longish doze, I awoke: my chaise was halted and my postilion had disappeared. After rubbing my eyes, calling out, shouting and swearing, I heard a violin a few yards away. The sound came from a tavern where some peasants were dancing, and my postilion amongst them, dancing with all his might.

At the stage before Antwerp I was unable, thanks to my rascal at Bruges, to pay for the horses, and on this occasion I knew nobody. Nor was there anybody who could speak French, and my rather bad German was almost unintelligible. I drew a letter from my pocket and tried to indicate by signs to the coaching-stage proprietor that it was a letter of credit on Antwerp. Since fortunately nobody could read, I was believed, and persuaded them to take me there, promising, still by signs, to pay all that I should prove to owe. At Antwerp I even had to borrow money from my postilion to pay a ferry. I had him drive me to an inn where I had several times lodged with my father. The inn-keeper recognized me, paid my debt and lent me the wherewithal to continue my journey. But by this time I was so frightened of lacking money that, whilst the horses were being harnessed, I hastened to the house of a commercial agent whom I had met at Brussels, and obtained from him a few more louis, although in all probability I should have no need of them.

At length, on the next day, I arrived at Bois-le-Duc. I was in most dreadful distress of mind, and for some time I had not the strength to get somebody to lead me to my father's lodgings. I had to take my courage in both hands in order to present myself before him. As I followed the guide I had obtained, I trembled at the just reproaches that might be levelled at me, and still more at the grief, and perhaps the sickness caused by this grief, in which I might find my father. His last letters had been heart-rending. He had informed me that he had fallen sick with the sorrow I was causing him, and that, if I prolonged my absence, I would have his death on my conscience.

When I entered his room, he was playing at whist with three officers of his regiment. 'Ah, so it's you!' he said. 'How did you get here?'

I told him I had come partly on horseback and partly by carriage, travelling day and night. He continued his game. I expected his anger to explode when we were alone.

After a while the company left. 'You must be tired,' said my father. 'Go to bed.'

He accompanied me to my room. As I walked in front of him, he saw that my coat was torn. 'That's just what I always feared would come of this trip,' he said.

He kissed me, bade me goodnight, and I went to bed. I was quite bewildered by this reception, which was neither what I had feared nor what I had hoped for. In the midst of my dread of being treated with a severity which I felt to be deserved, I would truly have liked, at the risk of some reproaches, a frank explanation with my father. My affection had been increased by the pain I had caused him. I would have liked to ask his forgiveness, and to talk with him about my future. I was eager to regain his confidence, and to have confidence in him. I hoped, with an admixture of fear, that we would talk next day with more openness.

But the next day brought with it no change in his manner; and some attempts that I made to bring our conversation round to this subject, some expressions of regret that I hazarded, met with no response. During the three days that I spent at Bois-le-Duc, we had no serious discussion. I felt that I ought to have broken the ice. This silence, which on my father's part was an affliction to me, was on my part probably wounding to him. He attributed it to an equanimity that would have been very blameworthy after such inexcusable conduct: and perhaps what I took for indifference on his side was really concealed resentment. But on this occasion, as on a thousand others during my life, I was halted by a shyness that I have never been able to overcome, and my words died on my lips as soon as I saw no encouragement to continue.

My father arranged for my departure with a young Bernese, an officer of his regiment. He spoke to me only of matters relating to my journey, and I mounted the carriage without having made a single utterance of any clarity concerning my escapade or my repentance for it, and without my father having said a word to me that could show that he had been sad or displeased.

The Bernese with whom I was travelling belonged to one of the aristocratic families of Berne. My father detested this government, and had brought me up to do the same. Neither he nor I then knew that almost all old governments are mild because they are old, and that all new governments are harsh, because they are new. (I except an absolute despotism, like that of Turkey or Russia, because in this everything depends on one man, who becomes mad with power; and in such a case the disadvantages of novelty reside in the man, although not in the institution.) My father spent his life declaiming against the Bernese aristocracy, and I used to repeat his declamations. We did not reflect our very declamations proved their own falsehood, by the mere fact that we could utter them without inconvenience to ourselves. They were not, however, always unattended by inconvenience: by dint of accusing oligarchs, whose only faults were monopoly and insolence, of injustice and tyranny, my father finally caused them to treat him unjustly; which cost him his place, his fortune and a peaceful existence during the last twenty-five years of his life.

Filled as I was with all my father's hatred of the Berne government, I was no sooner in a post-chaise with this Bernese than I began to repeat all the well-known arguments against its politics, against usurpation of the people's rights, against hereditary authority, etc. I did not fail to promise my travelling-companion that, if ever opportunity offered, I would deliver the canton of Vaud from the oppression of his compatriots. Just such an opportunity presented itself eleven years later; but by this time I had before me the experience of France, where I had been a somewhat impotent witness of what a revolution really means, as far as liberty founded on injustice is concerned; and I carefully refrained from any effort to revolutionize Switzerland.

What strikes me, when I recall my conversation with this Bernese, is the small importance that was in those days attached to the expression of any sort of opinion, and the tolerance that characterized the period. If one nowadays expressed one quarter of such views, one would not be safe for an hour.

We arrived at Berne, where I left my travelling-companion and took the diligence to Neuchâtel. That same evening I visited Madame de Charrière. She received me with transports of joy, and we renewed our Paris conversations. I spent two days at Neuchâtel, and had the fantastical idea of returning to Lausanne on foot. Madame de Charrière thought it a charming idea, since it would be a fitting sequel, she said, to my whole expedition to England. In reasonable terms, this would have been a motive for not doing anything that could recall this expedition, and for avoiding a performance that made me resemble the prodigal son.

So at last there I was, back in my father's house, with no other prospect than that of peacefully living there. His mistress, whom I did not at that time know to be such, took pains to make everything as pleasant for me as possible, and my family were very kind to me. But I had been there scarcely a fortnight when my father notified me that he had obtained from the Duke of Brunswick, who was then at the head of the Prussian army in Holland, a place at his Court, and that I was to make my preparations to go to Brunswick in the course of December. I regarded this voyage as a means of living more independently than I could have done in Switzerland, and I made no objection. But I did not wish to depart without spending a few days with Madame de Charrière, and I took horse to pay her a visit.

Besides the dog that I had been obliged to abandon on the road to Dover, I had brought with me from London a little bitch to which I was much attached. I took her with me. In a wood near Yverdon, between Lausanne and Neuchâtel, I lost my way and arrived in a village at the gate of an old castle. Two men came out at this moment with hunting-dogs, which hurled themselves on my little beast, not intending her any harm, but, on the contrary, out of gallantry. I did not properly understand their motive, and drove them away with heavy strokes of my whip. One of the men addressed me somewhat rudely. I answered in the same style, and demanded to know his name. Continuing his abuse, he said that he was the Chevalier Duplessis d'Épendes. After we had quarrelled for a few more minutes, we agreed that I should visit him next day, to fight him.

I returned to Lausanne and related my adventure to one of my cousins, asking him to accompany me. He promised to do so, but pointed out that by myself going to visit my adversary I gave myself the appearance of being the aggressor; that it was possible that some domestic or game-keeper had taken his master's name; and that it would be better to send to Épendes, with a letter to assure myself of the identity of the person in question, and after such assurance to fix another meeting-place. I followed this advice. My messenger brought me back an answer which certified that I had indeed to do with M. Duplessis, captain in the service of France, and was moreover full of uncivil insinuations based on the fact that I had made inquiries instead of appearing in person at the appointed time and place. M. Duplessis made another appointment, in Neuchâtel territory.

My cousin and I set out, and on the road were full of crazy gaiety. What prompts me to mention this is that my cousin suddenly remarked: 'It must be admitted that we are going very gaily to this appointment.' I could not help laughing at his taking credit for this to himself, who was to be only a spectator. For my part, I take no credit either. I do not claim to be more courageous than the next man; but one of the characteristics with which Nature has endowed me is a deep disdain for life, and even a secret desire to escape from it, in order to avoid whatever unpleasantness may be still in store for me. I am quite liable to be frightened by an unexpected event that affects my nerves; but, given a quarter of an hour's reflection, I become completely indifferent to danger.

We spent a night on the road, and were at the appointed spot by five o'clock next morning. We there found M. Duplessis's second, a M. Pillichody d'Yverdon, a French officer like his principal, with all the manners and elegance of garrison life. We breakfasted together: the hours went by, and M. Duplessis did not appear. We waited all day in vain. M. Pillichody was furious, and wore himself out with protestations that he would never recognize as his friend a man who failed at a *rendez-vous* of this nature. 'I have a thousand such affairs behind me,' he said, 'and I have always been the first at the appointed spot. Unless Duplessis is dead, I renounce him, and if he again dares to call me his friend, he shall die only by my hand.'

He was thus expressing himself, in knightly despair, when suddenly one of my uncles arrived, the father of the cousin who had accompanied me. He had come to snatch me from danger, and was quite astonished to find me conversing with my adversary's second, and my adversary absent. After further waiting, we took it upon ourselves to depart. M. Pillichody rode in front of us, and as we passed by M. Duplessis's estate we found his whole family on the high road, having come to offer me excuses.